# DRIFTWOOD ELLESMERE

# DRIFTWOOD ELLESMERE

*Volume One in the Driftwood Saga*

## JAMES DAVIDGE

ILLUSTRATIONS BY JUDD PALMER

BAYEUX

DRIFTWOOD ELLESMERE : *Volume One in the Driftwood Saga*
Copyright © 2006 James Davidge, *text*; Judd Palmer, *illustrations*;
David Lane, *cover illustration*

Published by: Bayeux Arts, Inc., 119 Stratton Crescent SW, Calgary,
Canada T3H 1T7, www.bayeux.com

*Cover Image: David Lane*
*Illustrations: Judd Palmer*

Library and Archives Canada Cataloguing in Publication
Davidge, James, 1973-
       Driftwood Ellesmere / James Davidge ; illustrations by
       Judd Palmer.
(Driftwood saga ; v. 1)
ISBN 1-896209-81-5
       I. Palmer, Judd, 1972-  II. Title.  III. Series: Davidge,
       James, 1973-  Driftwood saga ; v. 1.
PS8607.A78D74 2006         jC813'.6   C2006-903813-9

First Printing: July 2006
Printed in Canada

The publishing activities of Bayeux/Gondolier are supported by the
Canada Council for the Arts, the Alberta Foundation for the Arts,
and by the Government of Canada through its Book Publishing
Industry Development Program.

*Dedicated to my Grandfather*
*Barton Davidge*
*1923 - 2005*

*Special thanks to Natalie Norcross, Jyotirdipta Sen, Krista Russell, Steve Pearce, Bobby Hall, Eric Jordan, David Lane, Judd Palmer, Yancy Espinoza, Ashley Bristowe, Ashis Gupta, my parents, my brothers, my grandmother, and to my sister, Gillian Davidge, who introduced me to Ellesmere Island and so many other adventures.*

# Chapter One

The big is the same as the small, *thought Old Bart as he looked down at the shore of the Eureka research base on Ellesmere Island, the most northern island in the Arctic regions of Canada. Having been the owner of Eureka's Toque and Mitt Inn for the last thirteen years, Old Bart had walked the shoreline countless times. He knew its larger pattern. For the first time he was noticing that some of the little dents in the shoreline resembled the whole coastline. He could see a miniature version of what would appear on a map of the whole western side of Ellesmere Island right below at his feet.*

"*How fascinating,*" he said aloud as he pondered the wondrous dynamics of it all. This would not be the only exciting thing to happen to Old Bart today, and Old Bart was a man who had gone to the most remote land on Earth to generally avoid exciting things.

The elderly gentleman raised his wandering eyes from the tiny coastal replica and looked up at the vast ocean. He could see the white caps of distant waves come crashing down. Beyond that, the barren earth of nearby Axel Heiberg Island could be seen. These were familiar sights. In fact, Arctic water and desolate, ice-covered land constituted most of the images that one witnessed up here. A never-ending panorama of waves, more waves, snow and stone for all the eye to see. There was little else.

Old Bart watched as one crest of water rose and then crashed down. He was trying to find the rhythm of the ocean as he contemplated the relativity of erosion. He looked in the distance to *watch a far-away wave roll towards him. He looked for the top of a white cap but his eyes fixed on a distant object instead. Something was out there, and it was drifting towards him.*

*He watched intently as the object got closer. At first he thought it was a crate lost overboard from a cargo ship sailing the nearby Arctic Ocean. He then figured it to be a piece of scientific research equipment being used by one of the visiting scientists. However, when it got close enough Old Bart could see it was both what one would and wouldn't expect to see in the ocean.*

*It was a boat. This could be expected.*

*It was a rowboat. This would be less expected out in these waters.*

*Its only passenger appeared to be a pregnant woman. This was downright shocking to Old Bart.*

*As the boat washed ashore, he was there to meet it. He was greeted by a mix of shallow breaths and honest screaming.*

"Huh…Huh…      Huh…Huh…Aaaarh! Huh…Huh…  Huh…Huh…Aaaarh!" was all the woman could muster as Old Bart helped her from the boat. She immediately laid herself down on the rocky beach and put up her knees.

"Oh gosh." yelped Old Bart, "Oh geez…oh me… oh my."

Not knowing what else to do, he knelt down to hold her hand. She grabbed it. He was suddenly sharing her experience.

"Yooooow!" squelched Old Bart as the bones in his hand squished together.

The unlikely pair began to make a screeching symphony of sounds and words.

"Huh…huh…Eeeei!" she cried.

"Ouch…I mean keep it up!" he responded.

"Huh… huh…ooosh!" she bellowed.

"Oh my…good work…oh geez!" he yelled.

"Eiiii…ooosh…a-aaargh…ooosh… eeeeei… ooosh," she huffed and she howled.

"Well, look at that," observed Old Bart in

*amazement.*

*And soon there was a third voice, making burble noises and crying sounds.*

*"Waaaaaa!" wept the wee infant, brand new to this world.*

*"It's a girl," said Old Bart as he wrapped the baby in his coat and placed her on the woman's chest.*

*The woman looked at her daughter and cracked her first smile since she had come onto Ellesmere Island.*

*"I think I'll call you Driftwood," she whispered gently to her newborn.*

*Moments after her smile began, it abruptly changed to a more sickly expression. She suddenly grabbed Old Bart by the collar and forcefully brought him closer to her.*

*"You have been a kind stranger," she gasped, "and yet I must further burden you. I am not long for this world and I must make you promise me one thing."*

*"Waaaaaa!" wept the wee infant, brand new to this world*

*"What is it?" asked Old Bart.*

*He was holding the woman's hand again and could feel none of the strength that she had exerted a few moments ago. Her skin felt cold.*

*"Promise that you will burn my body. And that you will tell no one of how Driftwood came here. And that you will make sure that Driftwood is raised good and true. Please, promise me."*

*This was really more than one promise but Bart didn't want to argue. He didn't know what to say. He took promises very seriously and did not make them if he didn't mean them. For the first time he noticed that the woman was wearing a necklace that little Driftwood seemed to be grabbing at. The necklace had an amulet hanging at the end of it. It took a few moments but Old Bart recognized the amulet's images. They had meaning in the main world.*

*He suddenly understood where this baby had come from.*

*"By the fates," he whispered to himself.*

"I promise," he replied to the woman with sincerity.

"Thank you," she replied and then let out a final "Gaaasp" as she closed her eyes for the last time.

"Oh geez," was all Old Bart could say.

# Chapter Two

Driftwood looked out the airplane window as the snowy mountains of the Yukon turned into the green forests of British Columbia. It was her first plane ride. Old Bart had always told her that riding in an airplane was like riding a Phoenix.

"When you get off a plane it's like you have been reborn into a new place," he had told her.

*What a perfect way to spend my sixteenth birthday*, she thought to herself.

As the plane approached Vancouver, Driftwood was shocked as the forests and farms suddenly became gray boxes. She had never seen a city before. The regular blocks reminded her of the stark setting of her lifelong home, Ellesmere Island. She was already missing the forests that she had only seen from thousands of feet above and was happy that she wasn't staying in the city.

Driftwood felt quite lost when she entered the terminal. She had never been around so many people before. She did not even know who was picking her up. She kept telling herself not to worry as she glanced from one strange face to another. She started to breathe faster as panic set in. Moments later, her anxiety was fortunately relieved.

Holding a sign that said "Driftwood Ellesmere" was a young girl who looked about seventeen. The girl was wearing a pair of ripped army pants, a worn out plaid shirt and leather sandals. Her hair was a mixture of red dreadlocks and colorful hair weaves. She had a pair of sunglasses on with circular, red shaded lenses.

Driftwood had never seen someone her own age before. This girl was quite colorfully dressed compared to the brown clothes left behind by researchers that Driftwood had always worn after they had been tailored to fit by Clara. Driftwood was quite shy when she approached the sign-bearer.

"Hello, I'm Driftwood," she said quietly.

"Awesome! Nice to meet you!" the girl responded exuberantly. "I'm Marianne, but you might as well just call me Rose seeing as we're heading straight to camp. Let's grab your bags and head to the truck."

They made their way out of the airport and onto the highway. Driftwood couldn't hide her nervousness from being around traffic for the first time. She started to feel sick to her stomach but was able to fight it off. She distracted herself by talking.

"So, why did you want me to call you Rose," she inquired, "when your name is Marianne?"

"At Camp Magee we all have nature names," explained Rose. "It helps make us appear different from normal grown-ups to the kids. You won't even have to change your name if you don't want to. Driftwood is already a pretty cool name! Why are you named that?"

"It's what everyone has always called me."

"That makes it a name then. So, how did you get a job out at the camp?"

"My…guardian knows a man named Murph Magee. Mr. Magee's grandson is the camp director."

"Oh, you mean Swamp. That's wicked. Swamp is the best person to work for."

"Swamp?"

"Yeah. Like I said, we all have nature

names. Just wait until you meet the rest of the gang."

Driftwood was starting to get very excited about this curious new place she was going to.

"How old are you?" asked Rose.

"Well, I turned sixteen today," responded Driftwood.

"Today? You mean today is your birthday? Brilliant!" blurted Rose as she put on the brakes and pulled the truck off to the side of the road. Driftwood was confused by Rose's spontaneous actions. Rose pulled something out of her pocket. "I made this just this morning without knowing who I would give it to. It's perfect that today is your birthday! So…Happy Birthday!"

Rose started to tie some colorful thread around Driftwoods wrist.

"What is it?" asked Driftwood.

"It's a friendship bracelet. I guess that

means we're friends."

Driftwood looked at the beautifully woven item that now decorated her arm. It was a mix of green and yellow and blue thread twisted together in perfect pattern.

*Wow*, she thought, *my first friend.*

# Chapter Three

*Old Bart quickly gathered his thoughts and gently wrapped Baby Driftwood in his coat. He was careful not to trip as he hurried himself and one of the newest human beings on earth up to the Toque and Mitt Inn. As he rushed through the lobby, he tried to make sure no one could tell what he was carrying. He ran down the back hall and knocked on the farthest door.*

*"Clara! Open up, please!"*

*A voice came from the other side.*

*"Old Bart, if you woke me up to start my shift early, you've got another thing coming. I don't start cleaning for another three hours."*

"This isn't about work. Now, please, open the door!"

"What is it?" yelled Clara Kunuk.

Her door swung open so fast that a whiff of wind blew the few wet hairs on Driftwood's head. Clara was quite taken aback when she finally noticed Driftwood staring up at her.

"By the spirits!" Clara whispered almost to herself. "A child has made it all the way up to this barren land!"

She had lost all her anger from being disturbed and was looking at Driftwood with genuine eyes and her hand on her heart.

"Clara, I need your help," interrupted Bart. "This wee one's mother passed on while giving birth. I need you to make sure Driftwood gets what she needs while I deal with the dirty work."

"Of course," said Clara as she tenderly took Driftwood into her arms, "this rare jewel will be just fine. Would you like some milk, Sweetie? I bet it's feeding time."

Clara yelled down the hall towards the kitchen.

"Hey, Wilson," she bellowed as she covered Driftwood's ears.

"Yup?" responded a gravelly voice out of the kitchen.

"Bring me some milk. We've got a new mouth to feed."

"You betcha."

Clara and Wilson quickly applied the same care and attention that they put into the Inn to the tending of little Driftwood's basic needs.

Old Bart was handling the less direct needs. He gathered many of the logs that had been shipped in for the hotel's fireplace. He took them out to where the woman lay. The woman's rowboat was broken into many pieces and mixed with the logs to make a giant pile of wood. The woman's body was placed on it. With the help of a match and some oil he lit the hastily built pyre.

*A giant fire soon burned. Old Bart took off his cap and placed it over his heart.*

*"May your soul travel safely," he quietly said.*

*The woman burned to ashes with everything she had arrived with save her daughter and one other object.*

*Old Bart nervously studied the amulet as he walked away from the smoldering pile of ashes. He knew he was going to have to keep the necklace well hidden.*

*He hoped it would never be needed.*

# Chapter Four

Oh, the games Driftwood played out at Camp Magee. By the end of the fifth week she had become versed in many ways to have fun with children with nothing much more than an open field, some small ripped pieces of cloth and a bundle of energy. She had made a list of the games she could teach.

| | |
|---|---|
| Red Rover | Duck, Duck, Goose |
| Camouflage | Mafia |
| Johnny Whoops | Blob |
| Freeze | Ha Ka So |
| Wink Murder | Tax Collector |

| | |
|---|---|
| Capture the Flag | Don't Wake the Dragon |
| Magic Sticks | Human Knot |
| Itchy Minni Hoy | Run in Circles |
| Belly Scratchers | Giants, Wizards and Ghosts |
| Baloney Death | Bongo Bong |
| Ride the Rails | Lose Your Shirt |
| Rebel in a Pickle | and seven versions of Tag |

Driftwood had also ridden a horse for the first time. She had taken campers canoeing in the nearby river. She had led many hikes in the woods. The lush plants and diverse animals were abundantly exciting for her. So much of her environment had been just darkness and rocks before coming to the camp.

However, being a camp counselor was not all fun and frolic. Driftwood was solely responsible for the health and well-being of seven little girls. She had to make sure that they changed their clothes, brushed their teeth and didn't kill each other. She had to comfort young ones plagued with both nightmares and homesickness. She had to get them to activities on time and tend to at least three bodily wounds a day, usually afflicted by the simple act of tripping.

She loved every group she led. They all had stayed with her in the same small cabin. For the last forty-two years, every group that had slept in that cabin had been called the Falcons. Their name was carved above the entrance door. Over the years various people had painted falcons on all the walls of the cabin. It was easy to imagine that you were flying with them when you went to sleep. Driftwood loved her cabin. Every morning she and her campers would start the day with the cheer, "Fly, fly, Falcons, away!"

There were three other female counselors.

Clover was in charge of the Whitetail Deer cabin. She was from Vancouver. She took great care of her kids but was always a bit uncomfortable in the wild.

"I'm here to have fun, not get dirty," Clover would sometimes say.

Lichen led the Lynx girls. She was from Squamish, a town near Camp Magee. She was the camp daredevil. Climbing the steepest cliff, paddling the most unpredictable rapids were what Lichen liked to do.

Rose ran the Rabbit group. Although Rose had become Driftwood's closest friend at camp, it was still unclear where she was from. When asked, Rose would always say, "Oh, I'm from around," and then would proceed to change the subject. Rose was the linchpin of the camp. With her enthusiasm and tactful encouragement, she kept everyone going even when they were most exhausted.

There were also four male counselors.

There was Glacier and his Tortoise lads. Glacier was also from Squamish. He lived up to his name. He was big and slow but his intentions were always as pure and clear as ice.

Tide was the guardian of the Wolf cabin. He was from Prince Edward Island, on the east coast of Canada. Camp Magee was located on the west coast. Tide liked to say, "I may be a poor boy but I'm bi-coastal."

The Orca Whales had Wave as their leader. He was a surfer from Vancouver and was Clover's brother.

Stormy was the counselor for the Coyote group. Everyone used to wonder if he was either brilliant or crazy. They usually concluded that he was both.

Camp Magee had been owned by the Magee family for generations. Marv Magee, who everyone called Swamp, ran the camp with his wife, Marsh. Swamp's great great

great grandfather, Mick Magee, had won the land in a card game and made it into the camp shortly after. Swamp and Marsh took care of the ten horses and cooked the meals for everyone.

The sixth and final group of the summer was about to arrive. This was always the most exciting moment for Driftwood. The anticipation of giggles and chaos that the bus would bring grew with every week whenever a new group of campers was expected.

*This is my favorite part*, thought Driftwood, as the bus pulled up and she prepared herself for the usual scene of children barreling out of the bus with smiles and excitement.

When the door opened the staff was ready to welcome the normally hyperactive campers. This group of campers did not arrive with much energy. Instead, the kids stumbled out of the bus with their eyes down. They were not looking at the ground yet not a single one

Fifty-six kids standing around each other alone

of them looked up.

At first, Driftwood thought they were just shy until she noticed that they each had something in their hands. Each child was holding an identical toy that had a tiny screen and some buttons. They were all pushing feverishly on their individual boxes. Aside from the odd twitch, they were all practically motionless.

In a field that had been home to so many active and social games, there were now fifty-six kids standing around each other alone. The staff was stunned.

"Are those Talk 'n' Type machines in their hands?" asked a dumbfounded Driftwood.

"I don't think so," said Clover. "Those look like the new Mini-Entertainers from Great Blekansit Products."

"Well, it's time to put those pacifiers away, kids, and play some real games," quipped Tide as he grabbed a Mini-Entertainer from the closest one, a young boy named Adam.

Adam made a growling sound and snatched his toy back. None of the other campers had changed any of their expressions but you could see their knuckles tighten on all their machines.

"Holy Ma Joley," said Rose.

"Yup," agreed Swamp, "it's always a risk bringing kids out from the suburbs."

# Chapter Five

*Driftwood grew up in a strange place.*

*Where you are in the world determines how long your days and nights are. What season it is also plays a big factor. It is common for people to experience long, glorious days in the summer and then go through the grueling bouts of cold and lengthened nights in the winter. Most people have 365 sunsets and sunrises each in a normal year.*

*The inhabitants of Ellesmere Island are not those people. As the Earth rotates daily and orbits the sun yearly, the Earth's north side is closest to the sun from the beginning of spring to the end of summer. It is like if you rotated an apple in a dark room with only a single candle lit. If you tilt the apple towards the candle and spin it, most of the apple will go through light and darkness with each spin. However, the top part will always be in the light.*

*During the summer, Ellesmere Island would be near the top of the apple. It experiences one long day that starts in March and ends in September. The sun never rises or sets as it circles around the horizon. As the Earth, or apple, rotates, it constantly shifts its angle to the sun, or candle. Finally, the bottom starts being more in the light, as the South Pole starts towards its long day. In mid-November, Ellesmere Island begins a nighttime that lasts until mid-February. There are a few weeks of sunrises and sunsets between each change from constant light to never-ending dark and back.*

*In Eureka, where Old Bart had the Toque and Mitt Inn, he was the only permanent resident.*

*The other inhabitants, who were mostly scientists and military personnel, would normally stay for just a few months at the most. North of Eureka was a small military base called Alert that had no permanent residents. South of Eureka was Aujuittuq. Aujuittuq, which means "land of eternal ice," was home to a small settlement of Inuits. The Inuits were native to the land. They had been there since long before the arrival of research bases and military outposts.*

*Clara Kunuk was an Inuit from Aujuittuq. She spent her winters there with her family and summers in Eureka working for Old Bart. She and Wilson were his only staff and they both only worked during the seasons of light.*

*Driftwood's arrival did not change the length of days or night on Ellesmere Island, but she generally made the world brighter for the lonely lives she had entered. Old Bart, Clara and Wilson were dedicated to making Driftwood's a well-nurtured life for such an extreme location.*

The first summer that Driftwood had arrived, Clara took the most care of her. She fed her and changed her. When the long winter was arriving, Clara suggested to Old Bart that Driftwood come to Aujuittuq to be with Clara and her family. Old Bart refused.

"She'll be fine with me up here," asserted Old Bart. "This inn is her home."

Old Bart made sure Driftwood's room was full of light for the winter months. He set up her walls with shining stars made of tiny bulbs. She had her very own sun that hung like a chandelier from the ceiling.

There was seldom more than one or two guests at one time in the winter, so Old Bart could tend to Driftwood's needs quite easily. He carved toys out of wood, soapstone and animal bone. She had little animals, dinosaurs, fairies and fantasies made from the strongest materials to play with. They seldom broke and were easily repaired.

Clara and Wilson would return every

February ready to take care of the Inn and of Driftwood. Clara always brought back toys and books from her yearly vacation to Edmonton, the closest city although thousands of kilometres away.

Driftwood would crawl along the halls and stairways of the Inn as Old Bart would stand guard to prevent any accident. She became almost as agile as Bast, the hotel cat. She liked to do somersaults and walk on her hands. Eventually and naturally, she started to walk.

When Driftwood was six, Clara bought her a Talk 'n' Type machine. It was her only toy that required batteries. The Talk 'n' Type had a keyboard with big plastic buttons and a small screen. The mechanisms inside would bellow out a word in a digital tone. If you correctly typed the word that was spoken onto the keypad, the machine would belt out a short rewarding tune. If you spelled the word incorrectly it would emit a loud, burping noise. Clara had bought the

*Advanced Ninja Speller Edition. By the time she was nine, the little box had taught Driftwood more words than her three guardians combined. She just needed to learn the meanings of all the words.*

*For that she turned to the Encyclopedia Worldattica. A set of volumes printed thirty years ago, it had been at the Toque since Old Bart opened the hotel. The books had always been in the tavern but were moved to Driftwood's room in her early years. Before she knew how to spell or even what words were she had gone through every volume and looked at all of the pictures. With a little help getting started from her mentors, she had read all 40,000 articles twice before her tenth birthday.*

*Wilson taught her mathematics. He would spend hours in the kitchen with her, explaining fractions and measuring using nothing more than his flour cup.*

*Being in the darkest place in the world led*

her to journey to her imagination on a frequent basis. She had created friends out of the toys Old Bart had made her. She, Dulcina the Stick-Fairy and Murray the Mammoth-tooth Mouse, would play out in her vast snow and stone playground. They had climbed many snow-pile mountains that were almost as tall as Old Bart's truck. Along the rocky beach they fought handcrafted dragons and wood-carved saber-toothed tigers.

Driftwood was happy growing up. No one had told her how being at the end of the Earth should make you lonely so she usually wasn't. She had Old Bart, Wilson, Clara, the hotel guests, her books and her fantasy friends. It was enough for quite a while.

On Driftwood's tenth birthday, Clara and Old Bart created a scavenger hunt for their young prodigy to complete. Driftwood had to run around Eureka looking for everything from a white flower to something covered entirely in rust. She set off without hesitation. Old Bart *and Clara watched as Driftwood ran off into the compound. After a few moments of silence, they spoke briefly.*

*"Do you think she is ready?" asked Clara pointedly.*

*"Yes. Yes, I do," responded Old Bart pensively. "It is time."*

# Chapter Six

"That was the longest day of my life!" screamed Stormy as the counselors entered the staff cabin.

Glacier plopped down on the couch and let out a loud sigh that everyone could relate to.

"Those kids did not respond to one of our games," Lichen remarked despairingly.

"They wouldn't even go swimming," added Wave.

"One girl tried to bite me when I asked her to turn off her Mini-Entertainer," stated Clover.

Tide chimed in, "I've never seen anything like it."

"We have horses, canoes, bows and arrows," observed Rose, "they showed no interest in having a real experience. It's just not right."

As the counselors sat in a circle Driftwood was the only one that hadn't said anything. She had never seen much technology growing up. When she was nine, Old Bart had taken away her Talk 'n' Type when she had stayed up three days straight trying to get to the top level. Light switches had been pretty much the only other electric devices that Driftwood had encountered. Her experience with the Talk 'n' Type gave her some empathy for these kids. Her sympathetic feelings combined with her frustration. For the first time since getting to the camp, Driftwood burst into tears. She became embarrassed. Before coming here she had seldom been in a room with seven other people, let alone cry in front of so many. She didn't know what to do. Tears rolled down her cheeks as she sobbed uncontrollably.

She was calmed when Rose and Clover each put an arm around her. This gave Driftwood much needed support so she could finally vent her thoughts.

"It's so sad," she said. "It feels like these kids are losing their childhood. They don't even seem to be enjoying themselves. They just twitch and push buttons."

"That sounds like my dad at work," quipped Wave.

Stormy was getting angry as he roared, "That's exactly it! Those bigwigs at Blekansit are part of a massive plot to make everyone behave like robots!"

"It makes sense," considered Glacier. "They steal our imaginations as we repeat ourselves over and over and give them more money every time."

Everyone started to speculate on the machines from Great Blekansit Products that had infested their camp.

"They make their games hypnotic," recognized Clover.

"I read that these big gaming companies use psychological studies to understand children better," contributed Wave. "They create worlds that allow kids to escape anxiety and remove boredom. The result would have to be addictive."

"It's like a science," interjected Lichen.

"The science of games," mused Tide.

Driftwood started to regain her thoughts. She reflected on what everyone was saying. She realized that she perceived the world differently from her friends.

"It's not just a science," she said quietly.

"What did you say, Drifty?" asked Rose.

"It's not just a science. It's not just psychology and hypnotism."

Everyone was now listening intently to what Driftwood had to say.

"This is sorcery," she stated clearly. "These kids have had a spell put on them."

Stormy was the first to person to respond by asking, "What island did you say you were from?"

# Chapter Seven

Driftwood looked in her pillowcase. It was full of items she had collected on her scavenger hunt. She took stock of her bounty.

dryad (the white flower)    bottle cap

seashell    dirt clump

tin can    deck of cards

two willow branches    Mason jar with

five saxifrage petals    water mites

swimming in it

fourteen coins    postage stamp

shoelace strand    musk ox horn

rose rock    wolf tooth

*weather survey form*    *twenty five flat stones*
*seven animal hairs*    *and one completely*
    *rusted nail*

*She was running back to the picnic table from where Clara and Old Bart had initiated the grand quest. She was excited to show them that she had fulfilled every task.*

*When she got to the table there was nobody around. Instead, there was only an old looking scroll. She speedily unrolled it and proceeded to survey the contents. There was a map with a solitary poem written above it:*

It seems that we are nowhere
Yet always are we now here
Follow the signs with great care
And then you will be so near

*The hunt hasn't ended, thought Driftwood. She threw the pillowcase over her shoulder and* started to make sense of the map.

She was right beside the Toque and Mitt Inn. This was symbolized on the map clearly with a toque and, of course, a mitten. She was soon able to orientate the map. It was leading her to a spot marked with an X.

The X directed Driftwood to the top of Blacktop Mountain. This was a fair distance away. Driftwood went and got her bicycle. She would have to ride to the base of the mountain.

By the time Driftwood had arrived at the base of Mt. Blacktop she was exhausted. She jumped off her bike, collapsed on the ground and clutched her chest. That was the easy part, she reminded herself.

After she caught her breath she started up the side of the mountain. At the beginning of the ascent her body was resisting quite strongly. It was like every muscle was telling her to quit. She was having an internal battle as every footstep got her closer to the top. After about an hour and *a half she stopped noticing the pain. She was in a zone. All her brain could grunt was the simple thoughts of "top…soon…top…soon." Some clouds had kindly come in and were blocking the never-ending sun from over-heating her.*

This had better be a big surprise, *thought Driftwood as she neared the top. When finally she reached the peak she looked around the barren plateau. All she could see was Old Bart sitting at the other end of the summit. She dropped the pillowcase she had carried all this way and walked towards him. He was very unresponsive to her. He seemed to be concentrating quite hard.*

*She stumbled up to him just as her legs were about to give out. He did not move. She stood in front of him. He did not move. She sat before him. He did not move but he did finally speak.*

*"You've completed your scavenger hunt?"*

*"I did," replied Driftwood. "It took me a while to find the postage stamp but I finally got one from a research assistant."*

This had better be a big surprise, *thought
Driftwood as she neared the top*

"Driftwood, you are an amazing girl. At ten years old, you are more resourceful and intelligent than most grown-ups. You just biked a great distance and climbed a tall mountain. You have lived a lonely life and have never complained once. You have more strength than you could possibly be aware of."

Driftwood had never heard Old Bart speak about her like this before. The flattery made her forget her fatigue and listen intently.

"You have a strong knowledge of the world," he continued, "you know many facts."

"Like the capital of the Congo is Brazzaville!" blurted Driftwood. The compliments combined with the high mountain air were making her giddy.

"Yes, however, there is much you don't know about the way things are."

"What do you mean?"

"Driftwood, do you know what magic is?" asked Old Bart.

"You mean like pulling a rabbit from a hat?" responded Driftwood.

"That is a part of magic."

"Or voodoo?

"That is also a part of magic."

"What about fairies and dragons?"

"Those as well," affirmed Old Bart. "Magic is many things. Magic is everything. Magic is both a way to perceive the world and engage in it. Its paths can lead to inner peace and astonishing power. However, magic has many dark aspects and this had made it feared and disrespected. For centuries it has been chased away from everyday lives and relegated to entertainment and superstition."

Driftwood found the whole conversation quite confusing. "Are you saying you believe in magic?"

Old Bart returned to his state of concentration and bluntly instructed, "I want you to turn around and look across the valley at the highest peak of the Sawtooth Mountains."

Driftwood turned around. She looked across to the faraway peak. She watched and waited.

After fifteen minutes her impatience caused her to ask, "What am I looking for?"

Old Bart did not respond with any words. He instead started to emit a very quiet moan that seemed to come more from his stomach than his mouth.

Driftwood was about to say something again when she heard a rumbling noise. A wave of thunder was coming from the clouds. It seemed to echo Old Bart's groan. He suddenly moaned again, longer and louder. The clouds responded with a more tumultuous version of Old Bart's noise.

"How are you doing that?" demanded Driftwood. As she awaited an answer she noticed that the clouds had become quite opaque and ominous above the peak she had been told to watch.

*Old Bart let out one more grumble. He followed it with a pause and then a sneeze.*

*"Waaatchooo!" he cried.*

*"Ka-boom!" went the sky as a bolt of lightning struck the pinnacle of the Sawtooth Mountains. Driftwood was dumbfounded.*

*Old Bart finally spoke words again.*

*"Yes," he said, "I believe in magic."*

*Suddenly, so did Driftwood.*

# Chapter Eight

"Why are we doing this?" asked Tide. "It seems like a weird waste of time."

"Shhhh," hushed Rose, "we have to be positive if we're to help Driftwood."

"This is kind of strange," commented Clover.

"Come on, sis, it is pretty cool," justified Wave.

"I'm interested to see what happens," stated Stormy.

"I'm for anything if it helps us with these campers," added Lichen.

Glacier complained, "Do we have to sit

like this until she's finished or can we stretch our legs?"

"Quiet, everyone," whispered Rose. "Driftwood said we had to focus our energy towards her."

The camp staff had cleared all the furniture from the middle of the staff room. Driftwood had used a long tug-of-war rope to lay out a giant seven-pointed star. She had placed lit candles at all seven corners and then told the other counselors to sit cross-legged in front of each point. She was sitting in the center of the star with her legs crossed and her feet resting on their opposing knees. She had closed her eyes and had remained motionless since everyone had got into their positions.

The gang had managed to be quiet for five minutes. Rose was entirely committed to the process. This inspired most of the others to try their best to help out. Lichen, Stormy, Clover and Wave were all working very hard at their first known attempts at focusing energy towards someone. Tide complied by sitting at his point of the star but was dubious of the whole endeavour. Glacier was only able to focus on the pain in his knees.

He was momentarily distracted from his torture when Driftwood suddenly let out a mighty chant.

*Wisdom in and*
*Ignorance out*
*Spirits of the Aether*
*Please here me shout*
*Wisdom in and*
*Ignorance out*

Everyone aside from Tide was impressed with the performance. They were waiting to see what Driftwood would do next. Tide was rolling his eyes.

She let out a mighty "Oooomp!"

It was followed by a soft "Ah".

She then opened her eyes for the first time in quite a while. A smile grew on her face. The others all stared.

"I have been given a plan," Driftwood informed. "First, we must collect together hundreds and hundreds of pine needles that have fallen off of trees."

She grabbed a flashlight and headed for the forest.

The others were quick to follow, except for Tide who slowly sauntered behind and Glacier who took quite a bit of time to stand up as his knees had stiffened.

The group was able to scoop up many pine needles in little time. They all brought their collections to Driftwood. For the first time since getting to the camp she was not learning from her peers. She displayed a confidence that the others had not seen from her before. She was now leading them.

"Well gathered," she said with a glint in her eye. "Now, who is feeling stealthy?"

# Chapter Nine

"To begin with," informed Old Bart, "I will ask some questions."

His left eyebrow was arched up and he looked sterner than Driftwood had ever seen him look before.

"Who are you?" he queried.

"Driftwood Ellesmere," she replied, curious why he was asking her a question he already knew the answer to.

"Who am I?"

"Old Bart."

"Do you know who your parents are?"

"You know I don't. You always told me you

*found me drifting in the ocean.*"

"*Do you trust me?*"

"*You've been like my father although perhaps more distant than a real father would have been.*"

"*Many real fathers are distant, Driftwood. Again, do you trust me?*"

"*I've sometimes felt like you've always been keeping secrets from me. After what I just saw you do with the lightning, I realize that you have possibly hidden many things from me.*"

"*I kept things from you for your own safety.*"

*Driftwood now asked Old Bart a question.*

"*If something was threatening me wouldn't it be better if I knew about it?*" *she asked.*

"*You will learn, young lady, that knowledge does not generally provide one with security. Knowledge gives one power but it is also quite perilous. Let's move on to my next question. Knowing that knowledge is dangerous, do you still want to learn magic?*"

"Yes," she said without hesitation.

"Why?"

"Am I allowed to just say 'because'?"

"No. Again, why do you want to learn magic?"

"When I got to the end of the Encyclopedia Worldattica and read the final entry on the zygote, it felt like I had reached the end of information. I had complete comprehension of the wide world that I knew existed. All the encyclopedia said about magic was that one could cut people in half and float on a stage using smoke and mirrors. Now I see smoke coming from the Sawtooth Mountains that I think you just caused without any tricks. There is no mirror that big. You summoned lightning. Suddenly there is more for me to learn and I want to learn it."

"Then you shall have your first lesson. I want you to look again at the peak across from us. You see smoke from the brief fire caused by the lightning. The fire has stopped, as there is not much to burn on the top of these barren mountains. The lightning was caused by the water droplets in the cloud drawing energy from the earth in the form of electricity. Caught in the path of this massive drawal of energy, the little plants on the mountains burned because they were in contact with air, which has oxygen. So you know air, water and earth combined to make the fire. Fire often needs life and life can often be viewed as a kind of fire. Science generally studies earth, air, water, fire, electricity and life in measurable terms. It wants to explain everything as opposed to letting everything explain itself. Magic has always looked deeper at the forces of nature."

He then sat in front of her. "Repeat what I do," he instructed. He took a deep breath. His muscles tightened.

"Oooomp!" he bellowed.

"Oomp!" she echoed.

"Ah," he sighed as his muscles relaxed.

"Ah," she returned.

*They repeated this over and over again.*

*"Oooomp! Oomp! Ah. Ah. Oooomp! Oooomp! Ah. Ah," they chanted.*

*"Continue," said Old Bart as he stopped.*

*"Ooomp! Ah. Ooomp! Ah. Ooomp! Ah," she repeated. She started to time the noise with the blowing of the wind.*

*"Oooomp!" she would say as the wind blasted.*

*When the air current calmed she would say "Ah."*

*This excited her and she could not make sense of it until Old Bart spoke again.*

*"There are two forces that act underneath, behind and inside nature. One is the force of will or strength. This is needed for things to happen. It is impulse and action. That is the Oomp. The other is the force of imagination or idea. This is needed for things to change, grow and evolve. It is creativity and beauty. That is the Ah."*

*Driftwood was having difficulty trying to*

understand. This was not like learning to spell words or knowing the capitals of countries.

"Empty out your pillow case," Old Bart commanded.

She poured the contents out between them.

"Now I want you to concentrate," Old Bart told her, "Some of these items will be your first tools of magic. I want you to try and divine what you will first learn to use."

"Divine? What do you mean?"

"Clear your mind of distractions. Open your senses to the messages that the world is always sending you. Let the universe tell you your first tool."

Driftwood tried to clear her mind but was always distracted by a part of her mind asking itself if it was clear. Stop thinking, she thought to herself. It was proving to be a very difficult thing to do.

"This is impossible," she confessed.

"Just relax and let nature do the work. Be

*patient as it usually works very slowly."*

*She sat there frustrated for a few minutes. She then started to listen to the wind again. She was now hearing the 'oomp' and the 'ah' in every gust. She let the rhythm be the only sound in her mind. She was looking at a part of the Sawtooth Mountains across the valley. Her eyes were focused on a random cliff. Suddenly between an 'oomp' and an 'ah' she heard a distant crack. She did not have to move her eyes to see what happened next.*

*A small part of the observed cliff broke off the mountainside. Driftwood watched as it quickly shattered into many different pieces. She was ready to guess her first tool.*

*"The twenty-five stones," she said.*

*"Well done," confirmed Old Bart. "You learn quickly."*

# Chapter Ten

The counselors were now standing around Driftwood as she knelt in front of the large pile of pine needles. They were all outside, near the sleeping campers' cabins. Out of her backpack she took out a small satchel. From the satchel she pulled out four stones with a symbol scratched on each of them. She placed the stones around the needle pile. They each had a different symbol on them.

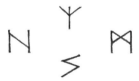

"These are druid rune stones," she explained. "I made them six years ago. They help me cast spells."

"Interesting," declared Stormy.

"I still don't buy it," said Tide.

"Then why are you here?" Lichen reasonably asked.

"To see it not work," Tide replied.

Driftwood took control again. "When I finish my spell, you will all know what to do. The quicker we act the more effective it will be."

She put her finger on the stone with the ᚾ symbol. She then let out a short chant in hushed tones:

*Hagaluz, ancient stone of hail*
*And natural forces of massive might*
*Disrupt this gripping and weakening spell*
*Found in the children's heads tonight*

She then put her finger on the ᛋ rune and said another hushed request to the ether.

> *Sowelo, rock of the sun*
> *Of life's forces both young and old*
> *Give us all your fueling strength*
> *Release these children from their toys' hold*

With her finger on the ᛗ stone she chanted.

> *Mannaz, the rune of mankind*
> *Please give these kids a hand*
> *Show them they're not alone*
> *That they truly share the land*

She finished with the ᛉ rune.

> *Algiz, the amber runestone*
> *Help us fulfill our parts*
> *Triumph over these electric traps*

*And win back the programmed hearts*

After a brief silence she quietly whispered, "Go."

Everyone grabbed handfuls of needles and made their way to the cabins.

"I can't believe we're doing this," Clover said to her brother as they approached her cabin.

"I can't believe how cool Driftwood is," replied Wave before they stopped talking to fulfill their task.

The next morning, Tide was the first to get up in the Wolf cabin. He wanted to make sure he had won his wager. He had bet with Wave that Driftwood's sorcery would not work. He expected the campers to freak out when they woke up.

The first camper in his group to wake up was Adam, the boy who had growled at him yesterday. Tide watched as Adam wiped the sleep from his eyes.

*This boy is going to go ballistic*, thought Tide.

Adam picked up his Mini-Entertainer and turned it on. His thumbs were already in position on the buttons as he waited for the machine to warm-up so he could play *Extreme Olympic Athlete*. He waited and waited but the toy didn't turn on.

*Here comes the growl*, thought Tide.

Adam stood motionless. Tide was watching intently. Adam kept looking at his machine expecting something to happen. He suddenly heard something from outside.

"Po-tee-weet?" was the sound that had suddenly grabbed Adam's attention. There was a bird sitting on a branch outside the window. Adam stared at the bird.

"Po-tee-weet?" repeated the bird.

This seemed to interest Adam. He put down his Mini-Entertainer and ran outside.

Adam watched as the bird flew into the sky and circled above him four times before flying off. He tried to follow the bird but eventually stopped to watch two squirrels chase each other around a tree. When the squirrels disappeared, he ran down to the lake to join Lichen, Stormy and more kids going for an early morning polar bear swim.

"I don't believe it," Tide said aloud as he watched the swimmers from behind a bush. He went back to his cabin to check on the rest of the Wolves. When he got there he was shocked to see seven Mini-Entertainers left on seven beds. When he looked out he saw kids playing everywhere. Rose and Wave were running a big game of Capture the Flag in the main field. Clover and Glacier were playing Camouflage with a group in the forest. Driftwood was making bead bracelets with some kids at the craft table. Tide came and sat beside her.

"So, uh, this magic thing," he stumbled, "what exactly did we do here? How did replacing the batteries with spooked up pine needles turn these robots into human beings?"

"We turned each machine into a phylactery," replied Driftwood.

"And what is a phylactery?"

"A phylactery is a protective amulet whose origins date back to early Greek civilization. I enchanted those pine needles. When we put them in the Mini-Entertainers, the toys each became a phylactery that could resist the strong magic emanating from them. When the kids picked up their devices the hold that had been cast onto them was dispelled. They were no longer in the grips of Great Blekansit Products. They are now the fun-loving and vital kids that they were always meant to be."

Tide surveyed the energy being displayed by these kids and smiled. "Well, I may have to do Wave's laundry this week," he said, "but I think I'm ready to say I'm happy to be proven wrong. I must say, Driftwood, great work. You did it."

"Oh, I'm not done, Tide," said Driftwood as a twinkle returned to her eye, "I'm just getting started."

# Chapter Eleven

"That's a ...an elephant," said an eleven year old Driftwood as she pointed to a piece of ice with her willow wand. She pointed to a bumblebee flying in the air. "And that is ...um...that is a meteorite."

The wand was two willow branches twisted together that flopped around like a piece of licorice as Driftwood waved it from thing to thing. She was following the instructions that Old Bart had given her.

"To understand things in a more complete way," he had begun, "it is important to escape the illusions created by the names we give things.

Today, when we go on our walk I want you to call everything something else."

"This is a rabbit," she said pointing to a rose rock. She was starting to have fun. She called a flower a lizard and changed Mount Sawtooth to an Egyptian pyramid. She waved her wand into the air. "Syrup is blowing all around us," she giggled.

"Very good, Driftwood," said Old Bart as he stroked his chin. "Now let us look back at the ice you first pointed at. You called it an elephant. How are ice and an elephant the same?"

Driftwood couldn't think of anything. She responded to the question by silence.

"Ice is made of water," Old Bart lectured. "Like with most living things, water is a major substance in elephants. Remember that science can help one understand magic. Now, how is a bumblebee the same as a meteorite?"

"A meteorite flies through space and a bumblebee flies through the air," answered

Driftwood, "and a bumblebee stings humans and a meteorite stings planets."

"Well done. Making connections is a very important skill."

"Old Bart, can I ask you something?"

"Of course."

"Does Wilson know any magic?"

"Why do you ask?"

"Well, you know all this amazing stuff and Clara has been talking to me about the Inuit spirits. But, when I learn math from Wilson in the kitchen he never talks about magic. When I bring it up he acts like he doesn't know what I'm talking about."

"Wilson cannot see magic," answered Old Bart. "He is marvelous at cooking from a recipe, counting things and fixing machines. But he cannot see the worlds and forces behind this one. Magic is in his blind spot. You, however, are continually opening your eyes wider and wider. Now tell me, how is a rabbit like a rose rock?"

*Driftwood stood up straight. "A rose rock is a crystal formation of minerals. A rabbit needs minerals to get nutrients. Also, rabbit and rose rock are both two syllables. And they both start with the letter R."*

"You're focusing on the name."

"Oops, sorry, Young Bramblebush," she said with a smile as she pointed her willow wand at him.

*Old Bart grinned slightly. He reached into his pocket, pulled out an apple and held it up in front of Driftwood.*

"What is this?" he asked.

"That is an... orange," Driftwood answered.

"Now, try to change it into an actual orange."

*Driftwood concentrated as her willow wand flopped in the direction of the apple.*

"That is an orange," she chanted dramatically.

*"It's impossible," she complained. "An apple can't become an orange."*

*Nothing happened.*

*"You're an orange," she commanded.*

*Nothing happened.*

*"Become an orange!" she yelled.*

*Nothing happened. She frustratingly looked at her flimsy sceptre. She wondered if it would ever do anything magical.*

*"It's impossible," she complained. "An apple can't become an orange."*

*Old Bart did not verbally reply to Driftwood's statement. He looked calmly at the apple. While taking in a giant breath he threw the red fruit into the air.*

*"Waaatchooo!" let out the old man. After his sneeze, he quickly opened his eyes and held out his hand. An orange landed on his palm.*

*"Nothing is impossible," advised the teacher, "and believing that is essential to achieving the most wondrous acts."*

# Chapter Twelve

"I can't believe we're actually doing this," said Rose excitedly as she and Driftwood got on the bus. "In eighty-seven short hours we'll be in New York City."

"Thank you so much for coming, Rose," Driftwood sincerely stated, "Great Blekansit Products has its corporate headquarters on the Wall Street and the Wall Street is in New York so I have to go there."

"It's said 'Wall Street' not 'the Wall Street'. So what do you plan on doing when we get there?"

"I haven't figured that out yet."

"Dandy."

"It's just after I saw what those machines had done to our campers I started thinking about all the kids in the world who have the Mini-Entertainer's spell cast on them. I have to try to stop that. The best way to do that is to go to the source."

"You know, Drifty, you're really quite brave."

"You're the brave one for coming with me."

"Hey, everyone else was going back to school. Why don't you have to go back to Ellesmere Island?"

"Old Bart is not my father," Driftwood exclaimed bluntly. "I can do what I want. What about you, what were you going to do if I hadn't asked you to come?"

"Let's look at the toy box to see if we can learn something," said Rose changing the subject. "Like they say, know your enemy."

On all sides of the Mini-Entertainer box was the letters GBP as the corporate logo. The three letters were drawn to look like three different animals. The G looked like the head of an eagle. The B was a spider's body. The P had the paw of a cougar or lion incorporated into it.

Driftwood studied the logo and then studied the name Great Blekansit Products. She suddenly noticed that if you took certain letters from the company name and rearranged them you could spell EAGLE, SPIDER and LION. She pointed that out to Rose.

"Wicked cool!" blurted Rose, "What else can you see?"

"If you take every odd letter in Blekansit it spells BEAST."

"Really?"

"And the two first letters in Mini-Entertainer spell ME. That might mean that the toys make kids think only of themselves."

"That's awesome that you can see this stuff."

"It's no big deal. After all, it's only their name. It probably doesn't mean anything."

Driftwood was thinking of the lesson about names that she'd had with Old Bart five years earlier. She suddenly felt a bit homesick and spent the rest of the bus ride thinking of her makeshift family on Ellesmere Island. Camp Magee had been so busy that she did not have time to think of home. Now, she was hoping that Clara, Wilson, Bast and Old Bart were alright. She wished she had phoned or sent a letter to them before going on her impulsive adventure.

A well-known fact about buses is that seventy-two hours on one usually feels more like seven years.

*If riding a plane is like being on a phoenix,* thought Driftwood, *taking a bus is like riding on the shell of a turtle.*

It felt quite different as they drove into the city compared to when she flew into Vancouver. The towers of New York were so massive. They were steeper and more daunting than the mountains of Ellesmere Island. It felt like the bus was entering a giant canyon or a never-ending labyrinth.

The two young girls disembarked from the bus.

"I think I've lost all feeling in my legs," complained Rose. "Well, here we are. What now, fearless leader?"

"I'm not sure," admitted Driftwood, "something tells me that we should just stand here."

"Fantastic!" Rose said sarcastically. "We came all this way and your big idea is to just stand here. It was sure worth spending most of our summer paycheck on the bus tickets."

The long bus ride had exhausted Rose's enthusiasm. She was about to continue her rant when she was interrupted by a loud voice.

"Driftwood!" a male voice called out.

"What the heck?" blurted Rose.

"Driftwood!" the voice repeated.

Driftwood looked around. She suddenly saw a familiar face in the distance.

"Wilson!" she called out. She ran up and gave the big cook a hug. She introduced Wilson to Rose.

"I can't believe it," observed Rose. "You pretty much knew only three people on earth before coming to camp and you run into one in New York City. What a coincidence."

"It's not a coincidence," said Wilson as he handed an envelope to the young magician, "Old Bart has sent me to deliver this package to you."

Driftwood opened the envelope. There was a letter and a necklace in it. Driftwood began to read the letter. Rose studied the necklace.

"According to this letter," said Driftwood as she read, "this necklace belonged to my mother. My mother? But Old Bart told me he never knew who my mother was."

"He probably lied to protect you," responded Wilson.

"Protect me from what?" inquired Driftwood.

"Uh, Drifty, you better check this out," interrupted Rose. The necklace was hanging from her hand. At the end of it was an amulet.

Driftwood took the amulet into her hands and studied it closely. She was stunned. Her whole world had turned upside down and inside out. On the amulet were three animal heads. In a triangle was the head of an eagle, the head of a spider and the head of a lion. Driftwood did not know what to say.

Rose tried to comfort her by filling the silence with, "In moments like this I usually like to say something like Holy Ma-Joley."

# Chapter Thirteen

"Every animal has a spirit," said Clara Kunuk, "Every plant has a story. Nothing exists that does not have a past. Most things have many different pasts coming from many different cultures. Do not let the contradictions of different myths cause you distress. Embrace the diversity of the legends for they are all true."

"All of them?" responded Driftwood with doubt.

"Yes."

"How can that be?"

"Ideas exist in many forms, each one great and limited. Accepting that people can have contrasting beliefs is an important step to achieving peace with the world."

"The vikings believed that the Earth came to be from the fighting of the icy land of Niflheim against the fiery realm of Muspell," ruminated Driftwood. "There is a Chinese legend that the universe was a giant, black egg that was cracked open by Pan Gu with his chisel to create the Earth and the heavens. Are you saying that they are both true?"

"Along with all other stories," confirmed Clara.

"You're beginning to sound like Old Bart," observed Driftwood.

"Well, he is also one of my teachers, sweetie," laughed Clara.

"Just like you're one of mine," said the twelve year old Driftwood with a smile.

"Yes, dear, and it is time to continue your lesson."

The pair was out on the rocky beach looking

out onto the open waters.

"I want you to look at the ocean," instructed Clara, "and tell me the legend of Sedna."

Clara had told Driftwood the story of Sedna many times. This was Driftwood's first time to tell it back. She felt quite nervous.

"Sedna was a young Inuit girl," began the young storyteller. "She left her family to marry a man across the waters. The man turned out to be a raven. Sedna was very unhappy when she found out her husband was a bird. Her father came to rescue her and took her in a kayak to paddle back to her family. The raven flew out to the ocean to stop them. He flapped his wings and created a violent storm. This frightened the father. He was so scared that he selfishly threw his daughter overboard hoping to stop the raven's storm. Sedna held on to the edge of the boat with both her hands. The storm continued. The cowardly father cut the tips of Sedna's fingers off with his paddle. The pieces fell into the ocean and became the seals. Sedna held on. The waves crashed about. Her father yelled, 'Take her! Take my daughter back!' as he cut off her fingers up to the second knuckle. The bits fell into the ocean and became the walruses. She still managed to hold onto the edge of the boat. The raven flapped his wings even fiercer. The father, more frightened than ever, cut off the rest of her fingers. These pieces became the whales. Sedna could not hold on any longer. She fell to the bottom of the ocean. She remains there to this day where she is the goddess of the animals of the sea."

"Not bad, sweetie," affirmed Clara. "You were a bit fast at times but, all in all, a story well told."

Driftwood liked telling the story. It made her feel confident and wise. She decided to ask Clara a question.

"Clara, do you know who my mother was?"

"You know I don't, dear. I've known you for twelve years. Don't you think I would have told you by now?"

"There are lots of things you haven't told me."

"This is true, but we can't rush your training."

Driftwood was suddenly hit with a possibility.

"Clara, do you think Sedna could be my mother?" she asked.

"Why would you say that?"

"Well, Old Bart always says he found me floating in the ocean. If she is the mother of all sea creatures couldn't she have created me? Can we ask her?"

"It is not wise to summon Sedna needlessly," cautioned Clara. "She sleeps at the bottom of the ocean and harbours hard feelings towards most humans."

"But it's not needlessly," explained Driftwood. "I want to know if she is my mother. Isn't that an important question?"

"To you, perhaps. To Sedna, it may just be an annoying inquiry."

"Fine. If you won't help me, Clara, I'll figure out how to contact her myself."

Clara knew Driftwood was clever enough and had the determination to do just that.

"Stand back, Driftwood. I will help you seek your answers."

Clara then held her arms out over the ocean. She held her head up high and began to chant.

"Takanakapsaluk Taleelayo," she repeated over and over again. As she spoke the ocean began to thrash and splash. "Takanakapsaluk Taleelayo."

The wind started to blow furiously. Driftwood held onto her hat as she looked out at the wild water.

Rising from the sea was a giant woman who had scales for skin and a giant fin instead of legs. Driftwood studied the hands. They had no fingers. The being had the angry expression of *someone abruptly woken up.*

   *"Who dares to summon me?" demanded the sea goddess.*

# Chapter Fourteen

Driftwood reread the letter:

*Dear Driftwood,*

*I am writing in haste. I have just spoken to Murph Magee's grandson. He told me of your last week at camp and the plan you had when you left. I'm sorry to have kept secrets from you, little one. I've made a mess of things. I only hope I can help you now. The necklace I've enclosed belonged to your mother. She died giving birth to you by the shore where I've always said I found you. Her last wish was that I raise you to be a good, true person and keep you hidden from your family. I still feel that I've succeeded at the first part. It seems like the second part of her wish might not last as long as I'd hoped. As I write this, fate is driving you closer and closer to your family. I have arranged for an old friend to guide you on part of your journey. Listen for The Laughing Man. He will sing of pretzels. I pray that this gets to you in time.*

*Be careful.*

*Love,*

*Old Bart*

Driftwood's head was spinning. Her crusade for justice had taken an unexpected turn. Her mother, who she had just discovered was long dead, could somehow be connected to Great Blekansit Products. The crowds of people in the bus station were making her anxious. She started to feel dizzy. Rose became concerned.

"Drifty, are you alright?" she asked.

Driftwood had the urge to sit on the floor in the middle of the station. She plopped herself right down, crossed her legs and closed her eyes. She started to breath, "Oomp!" and then "Ah" over and over again.

"Uh, Drifty," Rose interjected, "is this the best place to do that?"

Wilson made sure that no one stepped on Driftwood as she continued oomping and ah-ing.

Driftwood let out a long "Aaaaaah". She held out her breath and listened. The loud buzz of activity around her instantly disappeared. She heard total silence. She felt at home. She listened to the stark calm. This was something Driftwood had become good at over the course of her many years in near solitude.

Suddenly, a distant sound could be heard. It was hard to make out but it repeated itself enough that Driftwood figured it was exactly what she was expecting.

Laughing.

She jumped up and grabbed Rose by the arm.

"Come on, you guys," yelled Driftwood.

"Do we need to gather pine needles again?" quipped Rose as she tried to keep up. Wilson followed the two girls close behind.

Driftwood led them to the front entrance. The noise of the station had returned in her ears but she was sure she got them close enough. She looked around at all the people near her. No one was laughing. It was a bus station full of miserable people. She suddenly heard a quiet cackle behind her. She turned but only saw stern faces. She heard a giggle below her. She looked down. Sitting in the corner on the floor by the front entrance was a man in dirty rags. He had bags for shoes and a filthy beard that went down to his belly button. With trepidation, Driftwood approached the only person laughing.

When she got closer he started to warble a tune:

> *Pretzel here pretzel there*
> *Everything twisted like braided doughy*
> > *hair*
> *And with every bend*
> *You seem farther to the end*
> *But pretzel still there so I will care*

The man then looked up and stared with emerald green eyes.

"You must be Driftwood," he said in a friendly manner.

"And you must be the laughing man who sings of pretzels."

"Please, call me Hermit, for I am The Hermit of New York City," he said as he stood up and took an old fashioned bow.

"This is my friend Rose," said Driftwood.

"Nice to meet you, Hermit," said Rose as they shook hands.

"And this is Wilson," finished Driftwood.

"Who are you talking to, Driftwood?" asked Wilson. "Rose, why did you shake your hand in the air?"

Driftwood and Rose were confused.

"He cannot see me," explained Hermit. "Cannot or will not."

"Why is that?" asked Rose.

"Because I am too much magic and he is too little. His work here is done. Now, say your farewells and let us be off. I am to guide you to your destination."

Driftwood, Rose and Hermit left Wilson at the station and made their way out onto the streets of New York.

"Hold tight to your belongings," advised the hobo as he stroked his beard. "It is a stormy day for both the wind and the thieves."

# Chapter Fifteen

Clara and Driftwood suddenly found themselves surrounded by a gang of seals and walruses. A geyser of water was shooting straight up. At the top, sat Sedna, the Sea Mother. Her long tail fin waved in the air. Her arms were sternly crossed.

"Again, I ask," bellowed Sedna, "who is the foolish person who has awoken me from my slumber?"

"It was I," said Clara.

"But she did it for me!" interjected Driftwood.

"And who are you?" questioned the goddess.

*"A question? A question?" stammered Sedna.*
*"What is your foolish query, little thing?"*

"I am Driftwood Ellesmere and I want to ask you a question."

"A question? A question?" stammered Sedna. "What is your foolish query, little thing?"

"Are you my mother?"

"Are you a seal?"

"No."

"Are you a walrus?"

"No."

"Are you a whale?"

"No, I'm a human being."

"Then you cannot be my daughter for only sea creatures are my children."

"But I come from the ocean. I was found floating there. Is it possible you created me?"

"Child, it has not been possible for me to create since my father cut off my fingers. I can now only serve my sea animals. I don't have time to produce little children. Being a goddess is hard work you know."

Driftwood suddenly realized that she would

*get no answers here from Sedna. Driftwood started to cry. The goddess was taken aback. The last time Sedna had cried was when her father had thrown her off the kayak.*

*Sedna gestured to a pair of seals and then to Driftwood. The seals approached the young girl and within moments had Driftwood balanced on their noses. They carried her up to the top of the geyser and placed her beside Sedna. Sedna wiped the tears from Driftwood's face.*

*"Do not cry, tiny one," comforted Sedna. "We are much the same. Both abandoned children of the north."*

*"I do have people who take care of me and love me," sniffled Driftwood. "It's just sometimes I would like to know about my real family."*

*"It will happen, young Driftwood, but until then perhaps I can do something to cheer you up."*

*Sedna made a loud moaning sound. Soon a whale appeared at the bottom of the geyser.*

*"Jump on,"* said Sedna.

*Driftwood leaped down onto the whale's back. Sedna moaned again and the whale began to swim out into the ocean.*

*"Have fun,"* urged the Sea Mother, *"and make sure to hold tight to the spout when she dives under."*

# Chapter Sixteen

Driftwood had been in airports and bus stations but this was her first time on a city street. As the three made their way down the Avenue of the Americas, she was constantly distracted by everything around her. Stores, kiosks and merchant tables were in all directions. Glowing signs and endless windows towered above her. The street was swamped with trucks and taxicabs. The sidewalk was a flurry of people walking briskly to and fro.

"So much activity," she said in shock. "So fast…so busy…so many joyless faces."

"All cities are like this," stated Rose.

"How do people stand living in such an unnatural way?"

"Oh this is natural," corrected Hermit. "People are drawn to the city. They hope it will make their dreams come true. A lucky few achieve their dreams, or at least a dream. For many, dreams remain what they always were."

"How sad," commented Driftwood.

Hermit was stopped by a couple of teenagers. They were very skinny and looked like they hadn't showered in months. Driftwood was shocked to see young people living in such a state.

"Hey, Hermit," one of them said with a wave.

"Fellow outsiders," Hermit returned with a dramatic bow.

"Do you know where there's food?" the other asked. "We haven't eaten in days."

"Two blocks down and in the alley behind Fong's Grocery Store. Mr. Fong has thrown out some apples that were not fresh enough to sell anymore. I had three this morning for breakfast and they were a tad sour but still very tasty."

Driftwood really wanted to help the homeless pair but found that after buying bus tickets and travel food, she and Rose each had only twenty-seven dollars left. She knew that wasn't much money. She was surprised to see Rose reach into her pocket.

"I hope this can help," said Rose as she handed the teens a five dollar bill. Driftwood quickly followed with the same amount. Hermit looked displeased with the transactions.

"Thank you so much," the teenagers both replied. They then ran off to hunt for the apples.

The trio continued down the avenue.

"You didn't seem happy that we were giving them money," Rose said to Hermit.

"Bah to money," spat Hermit. "It is money that is the problem with this planet."

"What do you mean?" Driftwood asked.

"Money separates humans from the rest of the world. For most people, everything grows in stores as far as they are concerned. They have lost all connection with the systems that keep life on this planet going. Everyone seems to follow one command – 'Buy'. They think money will buy them happiness but it never seems to be enough."

"But everyone uses money," responded Rose.

"Not me," Hermit proudly affirmed. "I have not touched money in over thirty years."

"How do you eat?" asked Driftwood.

"There is plenty of food thrown away by the wasteful citizens of New York."

"Bah to money," spat Hermit. "It is money
that is the problem with this planet."

"Are you homeless?"

"I prefer to just say I live outside. All of New York is my home."

"Thirty years without touching money? That's pretty hard to believe," said Rose skeptically.

"And yet I have done it," responded Hermit, "and I've lived a happy life. Everyday is an adventure and my needs always seem to be taken care of. If someone tries to give me money I always refuse. If they insist I politely tell them to stick the money up their butt."

This made Rose and Driftwood laugh. They were starting to have respect for their hairy, homeless guide.

"When will we get to the Wall...I mean... to Wall Street?" asked Driftwood.

"Very soon," Hermit replied.

They were walking through a park. Driftwood saw something and was suddenly alarmed.

"A monster!" she screamed.

Rose laughed, "That's not a monster, Drifty, that's just a statue."

Standing before them was a giant bronze sculpture of a massive bull with intimidating horns and angry eyes.

"That is the Charging Bull," informed Hermit as they continued to walk. "It is the symbol of Wall Street. We are near your destination. Do you have the talisman?"

Driftwood pulled her mother's necklace out of her pocket. She had almost forgotten the telling gift that Old Bart had sent her.

"Excellent," said the magic bum. "Wearing that will gain you and only you entrance into the building. You must go quickly as there is a new security guard on duty for only the next twenty minutes. When you get past him take the elevator to the top floor. What you seek is up there. I have brought you this far. You must continue your journey without me. Be strong and wise, Driftwood. And remember, Rose cannot be seen going up with you."

Hermit gave a final bow and then started to wander away. He was laughing and singing again.

*When you see that old bull charge*
*Just be thinkin', it ain't that large*

Rose and Driftwood looked up at the building across the street from them. It was a tall tower with GBP in giant letters on the top.

"So," mused Rose, "do you have a plan yet?"

# Chapter Seventeen

"Happy fourteenth birthday, Driftwood!" yelled Wilson, Clara and Old Bart as Driftwood turned on the lights in the kitchen.

"Yaaaah!" blurted Driftwood as she tried not to spill the contents of the Mason jar she was carrying.

"Wow! Wow! Wow!" she exclaimed. "This is so nice but we sure are lucky I didn't spill my shrinking elixir. One drop and the floor would have changed to the size of a cracker. I was coming in to get some baking soda to neutralize my mixture."

Driftwood put the jar down on the counter.

*She added two scoops of baking soda to the liquid. Bubbles gurgled and popped. Both powder and potion soon vanished.*

*"Well disposed of, dear," said Clara.*

*"You should always remember to put the lid on the jar when you are walking with a magical potion," added Old Bart.*

*"What's everyone talking about?" a confused Wilson asked. He was often confused when the other three were all around.*

*"Make a wish before you blow out your candles," reminded Clara.*

*Driftwood closed her eyes. Since meeting Sedna the sea goddess she had thought often about where she came from.*

I wish to meet my family, *she thought to herself.*

*Driftwood felt a bit guilty making the wish with her adopted family all around her.*

*"Open your presents," suggested Wilson excitedly as he handed her a gift wrapped in*

colorful paper.

Driftwood unwrapped the package to discover a wooden flute. She had never owned a musical instrument before. She blew a few notes playfully.

Clara gave her a small bag of leaves. "These tea leaves can give you power over both the past and future," Clara explained.

Old Bart handed Driftwood a small object wrapped in leather. Driftwood unrolled the leather to reveal a Swiss Army knife. It had twelve different components ranging from tweezers to a magnifying glass.

"That is your sword," he stated, "it shall become the totem of your magical strength. Your willow wand has been your tool for mystical creativity. The twenty-five runestones that you carved three years ago give you a strong spiritual connection with the Earth. The jar is your cup. It connects you to the universe and grants you access to powers of the otherworld. These four items actualize your becoming a sorceress. Congratulations. You are now Driftwood the Mage."

Clara smiled, Driftwood blushed, and Wilson stammered, "Just what the heck are you talking about?"

# Chapter Eighteen

"That's your entire plan," confirmed a dubious Rose. "I drink some of the stuff in this old jar?"

"It will make you invisible," explained Driftwood.

"And how do I become uninvisible?"

"Adding salt and sugar to the potion makes it into an antidote," Driftwood said as she handed over two little bags, "but you must be sure to add both. If you only add salt it will become an elixir that will shrink anything it touches."

"And if I only add sugar?"

"It will make whoever drinks it fart for twenty-eight straight days."

"Who knows how that could come in handy, eh? After I become invisible what do we do?"

"You follow me closely to the top floor."

"Where we still don't know what we'll find."

"If you're scared you can borrow this," said Driftwood as she took out her Swiss Army knife.

"Sounds good to me," Rose said as she grabbed the tool. "Well, here goes nothing."

Rose took a couple of sips of the liquid.

"It's tingling in my mouth," she observed as her mouth began to fade away. "In fact, my whole body is tingling."

Rose started to disappear completely from view. Soon she was completely transparent.

"Now stay close," ordered Driftwood. "We only have a bit of time to try and get past the guard."

Driftwood walked up to the GBP building. Rose followed with her hand on Driftwood's shoulder. A doorman opened the very large and daunting front door.

"That part was pretty easy," whispered Rose. She always tried to be funny when she was nervous.

"Quiet," instructed Driftwood. She tended to become quite serious when she was anxious.

The duo approached the front desk where a uniformed man was sitting. The young security guard looked up and studied Driftwood. He seemed oblivious to the fact that Rose was also there. The guard suddenly noticed the amulet hanging around Driftwood's neck. He stood at attention and addressed Driftwood with a formal tone.

"How may I help you, ma'am?" he asked.

"Uh…I wish to go to the top floor,"

Driftwood responded.

"Of course, ma'am, just go to the elevator and I'll make sure it goes up there."

Driftwood and Rose walked to the elevator. The door opened. The pair walked in. They watched as the guard smiled and punched a few buttons. The door closed.

*That was too easy*, thought Rose as her stomach began to tighten.

A few minutes later an older man in a security uniform came to the front desk. The younger security guard was busy playing *Supercops* on his GBP Mini-Entertainer.

"So how was your first hour on your own?" asked the older man. "Did anything happen while I was having lunch?"

"It was pretty quiet, sir," answered the younger man. "The only person I let in was one of the Blekansits."

"Was it Hans or Harry?"

"Excuse me, sir?"

"Was it the father or the son?"

"Oh no, sir, it was a young girl. She had on the amulet that gave someone absolute clearance so I…"

The older man was no longer listening. He had picked up the phone.

Driftwood and Rose stood in silence as the elevator traveled up the building. To quell her own uneasiness, Driftwood began to breath her 'oomps' and her 'ahs'. She was hoping for wisdom. The voice of Hermit returned to her.

She could hear him say, "Stick the money up their butt."

*That doesn't help at all*, thought Driftwood. The elevator reached the top. Before the door opened, Driftwood turned to her closest friend.

"Thank you so much for coming with me, Rose," she said softly. "Just because you're invisible doesn't mean I don't need you."

"I know, Drifty," replied Rose. The kind words helped loosen the knots in her stomach.

The elevator doors slid open. The two girls looked out into darkness. Driftwood reached into her pack and pulled out her flashlight. She shone the beam into the unlit room. The room was so big that the light did not go to the end.

"Should we go in?" asked Rose. Just as she was asking the doors started to slide shut. Rose pushed Driftwood out of the elevator just as the doors closed behind them.

"Rose, are you still there?" whispered Driftwood. "I've dropped my flashlight. I can't see anything."

"Still here, partner," responded Rose as she stumbled around looking for a light switch.

Before they could speak again a loud noise came from the far end of the room.

"Ka-roar!"

*The switch must be here somewhere*, thought Rose trying not to let the shrill sound bother her.

"Ka-roar! Ka-roar! Who goes there?" yelled a squawky purr-like voice.

Driftwood reached into her pack and pulled out her willow wand. She held out the floppy sceptre and tried to maintain a brave and confident face. She was scared but didn't want to show it. Rose finally found the switch. A giant chandelier cast a bright glow onto a humongous room.

Driftwood was standing at the foot of a massive cobweb, almost as big as the entire room. At the back and top of the web was a giant creature. It had an eagle's head and wings, a huge spider's body and eight lion legs coming from it. The monster was both frightening and beautiful. Behind it were a bunch of objects wrapped in the webbing.

"Ka-roar! The light! Ka-roar!" screamed

the beast.

It tried to cover its eyes with its two front paws. The other six paws started to crawl towards Driftwood.

"For disturbing my lair you will be pecked, scratched and wrapped! Ka-roar!"

# Chapter Nineteen

"You're not the boss of me, Old Bart!" yelled Driftwood at her mentor. "I've been fourteen for months now. I think I'm old enough to choose to have a day off of lessons."

"One must work to gain success," the old sorcerer responded. "A few hours a day is all that is required."

"How can you say that daily practice is required when it has been night since September? Maybe I need a break every now and again. And not just when you say but when I want!"

Driftwood and Old Bart had been arguing a lot since the sun set for the final time that year. It was now late December and the two were usually sparring over something or another when they were together. They had always enjoyed happy winters before this. Guests were infrequent so they were often each other's only company during the season's long night. The absence of Wilson and Clara had always made the bond between the young girl and old man stronger. However, this winter it seemed like all the bonds made over fourteen years were being severed due to various conflicts between them. They would fight over small things like what time it was or whose turn it was to do the dishes. Driftwood spent most of her time in her room. Sometimes she would read and wonder. Other times she would play her flute for Bast the Cat. And then there were moments when she would just sulk.

After the two would argue Driftwood was always filled with regret. She would tell herself not to get mad at Old Bart again but when next they would meet it would always end with *yelling. She was frustrated that she seemed to have no control over her isolated situation or her tumultuous feelings.*

*"You are confused over what you want," Old Bart finally responded. "You have said that you want to be a magician but now you don't want to respect the discipline."*

*"I respect magic," retorted Driftwood, "I focus, study, and work at it all the time but it never seems to be enough. If magic is supposed to be about freeing my perceptions why does it require so much structure? Sometimes I think that it's not magic that demands so much of me but it's just you that makes the demands."*

*Driftwood chose this moment to end the discussion and retreat to her room.*

*As usual, Old Bart found himself standing alone in the Toque and Mitt Inn, feeling a sense of frustration and regret more similar to Driftwood's than either of them would guess. He did not know how to avoid their inevitable arguments. Driftwood still needed more training but was showing ever-growing resistance towards Old Bart's expectations.*

*"She is still young," he reminded himself, "and perhaps I have been too hard on her."*

# Chapter Twenty

"I will eat you for invading my home," the monster cried to Driftwood.

The beast swung one of its mighty paws at the young girl. Driftwood jumped clear of the attack. She landed on part of the web. The web was a combination of silk and wires. She noticed that the strands weren't just attached to the walls but actually went into them.

"What are you?" asked Driftwood.

"I am an Eaderion and you have disrupted the creation of one of my inventions. Ka-roar!"

"Your inventions?"

The Eaderion used one of its paws to point to the wrapped bundles at the back of its web and another leg to strike at Driftwood again.

It explained proudly, "I spin one new game, device or gadget every hour. Your abrupt arrival is preventing me from finishing my latest work of brilliance."

Driftwood did a somersault to dodge the second blow.

"And what was it to be?" she inquired.

"A gadget that butters your toast."

"But people don't need that. It takes two seconds to spread butter on toast."

"They don't need the machine. Ka-roar! But they'll want it."

"Why?"

"Because humans love time. More devices that give them more free time will always be demanded. My butter spreader will give them the extra time they desire. With my web I am networked to every computer and television in every home in the world. I see what people watch and where they go with their TVs and microprocessors. Everyone wants the same thing. More time to watch their shows and surf the net."

The speech had slowed the Eaderion's assault. It was usually alone and was relishing the chance to talk about itself.

"I have never watched TV or been on a computer," stated Driftwood. "Is it really what most people want to do?"

"It provides entertainment. Every game a person plays or program they watch makes the world more fun for them. They feel like they have done something when really they have done nothing at all. It's quite marvelous."

"It is evil. You create devices that cause both people's bodies and minds to cease operating. You create spells that turn people off and you must be stopped."

Driftwood pointed her wand boldly at the mystical creature.

"You're a stale loaf of bread," she commanded.

Nothing happened.

"Ka-roar! Your magic doesn't seem to be working, little girl."

The Eaderion swayed another leg at Driftwood. This time it connected with Driftwood's pack. The young mage tumbled as the pack was thrown clear across the room.

"You're a squished banana," Driftwood said as she tried to regain her balance on the web.

The Eaderion turned its body around. Its head was still facing Driftwood as it lifted up its backside. A stream of web shot out a tiny hole. Driftwood dove clear of the silky bolt. Another strand shot out. This time it hit one of Driftwood's feet. She couldn't move.

"You're a rotten tomato," was her only

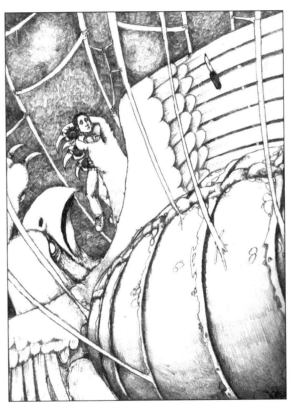

"I will eat you for invading my home,"
the monster cried to Driftwood

defense.

Again, nothing happened.

The colossal creature turned around. It picked up Driftwood with its two front paws and pulled her up to its head.

"Do you have any last thoughts before you become my dinner," inquired the beast, "seeing as your words have proven to be quite harmless?"

Again, Driftwood raised her wand. A slight grin was growing on her face.

"You're…well, I mean you've …uh…I guess I'll just say it."

"What? Ka-roar!"

"You've been distracted."

"Distracted? Distracted from what?"

"From me," announced Rose from the top of the web.

"Who said that?" demanded the monster. It turned around. It could not see the ghostlike Rose but it did see a shocking sight.

"My web!" it screamed. "My wonderful, wonderful web! What have you done?"

All but the strands touching the floor and three lines up top had been cut while the fighting had ensued.

"It looks like you're about to be disconnected," replied Rose as she swiped one more top strand with the Swiss Army knife. It snapped away and made a sound like a breaking violin string.

"No, stop!" pleaded the Eaderion.

Another strand snapped. The web was wobbling as it pivoted on one final string. Rose was holding onto it with one strong hand.

"Here goes," said Rose as she cut at the last line. The whole web collapsed to the ground.

"Uuugh," blurted Rose as she struck the ground.

"Eeeeii!" cried the Eaderion as it fell.

It tried in vain to stay up with its wings but they had been unused for so long. When it landed it lost its hold onto Driftwood. Driftwood looked for her pack. It was nowhere near her. She reached into her pocket. She pulled out a ten, a five and seven one dollar bills. As she studied the wad of paper she again heard Hermit saying, "Stick the money up their butts."

"I'll get you for this," bellowed the monster as it grabbed for Driftwood. Driftwood ducked and crawled under the body of the Eaderion. She looked for the little hole that had shot the webs. She did exactly what Hermit had advised.

"You shall not escape," the creature threatened. It raised its backside again. However, instead of producing more web the back of the beast expanded like a balloon. The Eaderion looked quite concerned.

"Oh no," it sighed. The swelling started

to contract. Webbing started to gush out of its beak. The great beast collapsed. A river of silk and spit oozed out of its mouth. It was followed by a butter knife with a tiny mechanical hand holding it.

Driftwood stood up. She studied the Eaderion. Its eyes were closed and it had stopped moving.

"Your wicked web and malevolent machines have been stopped," she said triumphantly.

Her satisfaction of defeating such a horrible thing was interrupted by a voice from the elevator.

"The Eaderion!" yelled a pony-tailed young man in a black suit from the elevator.

He ran towards the collapsed creature and clutched its head.

The young man cried, "Father, it's been destroyed."

As he spoke, the two security guards ran

out of the elevator and grabbed Driftwood by the arms. Following them out was a bald man wearing another black suit.

"Be calm, Harry, our intruder is still with us," instructed the bald man. "Spiton, see to the inventions in the back."

*Did he just call someone 'spit on'?* wondered Driftwood.

"Of course, master," said a grumbly voice. A short, gray-haired, wrinkled and hunched-over man came out of the elevator. He meekly scurried over to the wrapped bundles and gathered them into his arms.

The bald man was clearly in charge. He studied Driftwood. His eyes were dark as they stared at her. Driftwood found him more frightening than the Eaderion.

"And who might you be?" interrogated the bald man.

"My name is Driftwood Ellesmere. I came here to stop a maker of soul-trapping machines and I have succeeded," a defiant Driftwood replied.

"We'll just have to raise the next Eaderion a little more quickly than planned," her interrogator said smugly as he studied the necklace around Driftwood's neck "Now tell me before I have you arrested. How did you get this amulet?"

"It belonged to my mother."

"Your mother? Your mother is Eva Wood Blekansit?"

"I didn't know my mother's name. She died giving birth to me."

"She is dead?" the man asked sorrowfully. "All these years I hoped she was still alive."

The bald man started to weep. With a wave of his hand he commanded, "Release the girl."

The two guards let Driftwood go. The bald man suddenly gave her a big hug. He held her tight. Driftwood was stunned.

"If that amulet belonged to your mother then that makes you my daughter. My name is Hans. Welcome to the Blekansits."

Driftwood was finally reunited with her family. She knew she should have been happy.

Instead, all she could feel was a sharp part of the amulet being pressed painfully into her chest.

# Chapter Twenty-One

Bast the Cat was quite alarmed as Driftwood frantically paced around her bedroom. Driftwood was pointing her willow wand at various things.

"You're a toadstool," she commanded to her lamp.

Nothing happened.

"You are a treasure chest full of gold and jewels," she told her desk.

Nothing happened.

"You're a suit of armor," she stated to a shirt that was lying on the ground.

Nothing happened.

She left her room in a huff. She searched throughout the hotel for Old Bart. He was finally found in the kitchen finishing a sandwich.

"I am sick and tired of this stupid wand!" she exclaimed as she threw the woven willow branches onto the floor. "At my birthday you said that it was the source of my mystical creativity yet in the four years since I made it I have never ever been able to actually do anything with it. It's just a dry, wilted and useless piece of a plant."

"Well, perhaps it should go into the compost bin if that is what you would like," suggested Old Bart. "It will not be useless there."

Old Bart's comment made her feel guilty as so many of his statements recently had. She resented that every time she expressed herself, he acted like she was giving up and quitting. She decided to pick up the wand in an attempt to regain her composure.

"How can my wand be a magical tool if it doesn't do anything?" Driftwood asked. "Aren't tools supposed to do things?"

"The wand has been an outlet for some of your creativity. The renaming exercise helps you explore deeper ideas of abstract connectiveness. This will manifest as great power when you have figured out how to find your focus."

"And how do I do that?"

"Let's see how you are doing," Old Bart said as he opened the door to the walk-in cooler.

He went into it and emerged a few moments later with an apple in his hand.

"I want you to concentrate but also relax," he instructed. "Remember your 'oomps' and 'ahs'. Now, try and change this into an orange."

Driftwood pointed the wand at the apple and took in a deep breath of air.

"Ooomp!" she let out followed by, "aaah."

She stared at the red apple and tried to imagine it changing form.

An orange and an apple are both ball-shaped fruits, *she reminded herself.*

# Chapter Twenty-One

"You're an orange," Driftwood commanded to the apple.

Nothing happened.

"You're an orange! You're an orange! You're an orange!" yelled an exasperated Driftwood.

Nothing happened.

"You are clearly not relaxing," observed Old Bart, "and I highly doubt you are concentrating."

"Then tell me how!" demanded Driftwood.

"Finding focus is not something I can just explain to you. It is a journey that you must discover for yourself. You must be patient. When the epiphany comes it will be both subtle and obvious. You must both wait for it and search for it."

"I'm tired of your riddles," complained Driftwood. "What good are you as a teacher if I can't understand or make use of what you say?"

As usual, after Driftwood insulted Old Bart, she ran up to her room and locked her door. She shoved her head into her pillow and screamed for seven seconds straight. She screamed out of anger and guilt.

She felt like a failure who couldn't do anything right.

# Chapter Twenty-Two

"You did the right thing coming and seeking me out," Hans Blekansit said to Driftwood. "However, it is unfortunate that you felt it necessary to kill the Eaderion to get my attention."

Driftwood decided not to tell him that destroying the beast had been her actual mission. Being united with her father and brother was a very unexpected coincidence. She decided to change the subject.

"Where are we flying to?" she inquired.

"In a matter of minutes, this jet will have us at our home on Grand Cayman Island."

"Why do you live there?"

"Two reasons, my daughter. First, it is very warm. Second, they don't have any taxes. I get to keep every cent that I make and I make a lot of cents. Great Blekansit Products is one of the largest companies in the world."

"And we don't have to do anything," chimed in Harry Blekansit as he took a sip from a drink that Spiton had just made for him, "it just happens."

"Would you like anything, Master?" Spiton asked Hans.

"I'll have my usual Bloody Mary," he replied.

"And for you, m'lady?" Spiton directed to Driftwood.

"Do you have apple juice?"

"Of course."

At the back of the jet the old servant prepared the cocktails and carried them on a tray down the aisle. He suddenly lost his balance. The tray flew out of his hands. The drinks spilt everywhere. A tiny drop landed on Hans's cuff.

"Spiton, how dare you?" barked Hans. "You have destroyed my outfit!"

"A billion pardons, Master. I seemed to have tripped on something."

Rose tucked her legs in closer to her seat. She had almost revealed her presence.

Just as Spiton finished cleaning up the mess, they were landing on a private airstrip.

*That was fast*, thought Driftwood, *if flying on a plane makes one reborn perhaps jet travel changes one completely.* After all, it had turned out her name should now be Driftwood Blekansit. She kept saying it over and over again in her head, wondering if it would ever feel right.

The group disembarked from the jet directly into a long limousine. They drove through a forest of palm trees. Driftwood was in awe of all the exotic plants and animals. She had seen six different kinds of lizards in the trees and flowers that bordered the narrow road. The jungle turned into a sandy beach. To Driftwood's left was a magnificently emerald and blue ocean. She could tell that this sea was full of more life and activity than the cold of her homewaters had ever allowed. She looked to the right to be greeted by a large white mansion adorned with many pillars, patios and marble statues. It looked about eighteen times the size of the Toque and Mitt Inn.

"This is Blekansit Manor," welcomed Hans. "It shall be your new home."

Upon hearing that, Driftwood began to feel a bit queasy.

"Come, my daughter," he said as they got out of the limousine. "I shall give you a tour."

They entered the mansion into an enormous front hall. In the centre of the hall were three giant statues. One of them was of

In the centre of the hall were three giant statues

Hans and another was of Harry. The third was of a man who looked similar to Hans but a bit older with a goatee on his chin.

Hans pointed to the other statue and explained, "This is a statue of my father, Heinz Blekansit. All three of these statues are made of solid gold. It cost millions of dollars to cast them."

Hans then showed Driftwood an elegant dining room, a well stocked gaming room, a library with thousands of unread volumes, and at least thirty-three other rooms of various description. Harry followed close behind, jealous of the attention his newfound sister was receiving. He vented his frustration by knocking over every statue they walked by. Before crashing on the ground, the marble icons were all diligently caught by Spiton and returned to their upright positions.

They walked outside to the back of the mansion.

"Was that all the rooms?" an overwhelmed Driftwood inquired.

"That was merely a quarter," Hans arrogantly answered. "We have come outside to check on something."

They walked down a path towards a massive pit in the ground. A waist-high fence surrounded it. Emanating from the bottom was a soft wailing sound. Driftwood put her hands on the rails and looked over. She was taken aback by what she saw.

Crawling around on eight legs was a tiny creature with a body that resembled a furry bread loaf. It was flapping its wings to no avail as it pecked the ground with its wee beak.

"Ka-purr," it wailed.

"A baby Eaderion," Driftwood alarmingly observed.

"Yes, fortunately born just a few months ago from the beast you destroyed," informed Hans. "An Eaderion lives an average of twelve years. When it is seven it produces its only offspring. At the age of five it is usually old enough to succeed its parent as our inventor. We'll have to feed this one some steroids and growth hormones to speed up its development. Spiton, I want you to get on that right away. Contact the chicken and cow industry. They know how to speed up the growth of animals."

"As you wish, Master," obeyed the aged lackey who hastily made his way back to the manor.

"Where do these beings come from?" probed a curious Driftwood.

"Many years ago, Heinz Blekansit, a magician and businessman, was working in his office to create a Griffon," began Hans. "This was an ancient being that granted its keeper great power. It had the front of an eagle and the back of a lion. My father had acquired the two animals with the intent of combining them. While he was performing the merging incantation, a spider had lowered itself from the ceiling to a position between the lion and eagle. When he cast his spell the three creatures merged to become an Alchemical Chimera. My father was elated. Chimeras were creatures of even greater legendary might than Griffons. He watched as the infant invention, named Eaderion by him, crawled around his desk with its eight feline feet as it searched for its first food. It snatched a calculator with its beak and quickly chewed the machine down. It devoured the dictionary that had sat on my father's desk for years. It then ate his telephone and began to spin a web made of silk and wires. After about an hour it produced an object out of its web hole. It was a tiny plastic disc with a transparent top. There was a little maze with a marble in it. The goal was to get the marble from one end of the labyrinth to the other. The maze was cleverly designed to make it look possible to get to the other side. However, no matter how long a person tried, the marble always ended up back where it started. It was an impossible puzzle, a glorious waste of time and an extremely popular toy. It was your grandfather's first success in business. The Eaderion had become his secret weapon in a world where ideas were of the highest value. Every device that the beast produced created more wealth."

"Did your father teach you magic?" inquired Driftwood.

"He had no time," Hans replied appearing quite disturbed. "It took all his efforts to build his corporate empire. When I was nineteen he and my mother both died in a plane crash. I inherited their wealth, their property and the two Eaderion beasts that were alive at the time. I now run the largest gadget and game company in the world. The only magic I need comes from the inexhaustively inventive Eaderions. Unlike my father, I take time out of my busy schedule to teach Harry what I know."

"And what do you know?"

"Basically, how to tell people to do things."

Harry picked up a rock and threw it at the little Eaderion.

"Take that!" he yelled with a sick grin on his face.

"Ka-yipe! Ka-grrr!" screamed the small, mystical animal.

"What did you do that for?" demanded Driftwood of her smug looking sibling.

"Let your brother be," instructed Hans. "It is important that the Eaderion have a fear and distrust of humans before it is connected to its globally networked web."

"Why is that?" asked Driftwood.

"It requires hate to build its enchanting

inventions. It focuses its anger on creating enchanting manipulations that entrap humans."

Harry threw more rocks. The Eaderion tried to shield itself with its many legs.

Driftwood was taking a quick dislike to her brother. Turning away from the violence she tried to find solace in a nearby garden. She looked at some roses and was reminded of her ghostly friend. She hoped Rose was all right.

Rose had made her way to the top level of Blekansit Manor. She had walked by many maids and butlers without a single one noticing. At the end of the hall she found an entrance to the attic. People always hide things in attics. She waited for all the staff to leave the floor. When the coast was clear she went into a nearby room and grabbed a chair. She used it to boost herself into the upper space.

The attic was very dark and outrageously dusty. It was full of junk and cobwebs. Rose waded through a sea of baby toys and outdated outfits. Her toe made hard contact with the base of a wooden trunk. She clenched her teeth to keep herself from screaming. An inspection of the crate revealed a baggage tag with the name "Eva Wood Blekansit" on it. She soon had the trunk unlatched and open.

As her hands swam through a sea of old clothes and shoes, she suddenly felt something small and rectangular at the very bottom.

*Jackpot*, thought Rose.

She brought the item out to discover that it was a diary. When she opened it to the first page, there was an article with a picture of a woman that looked like an older Driftwood. Rose read the headline.

"Holy Ma-Joley," uttered Rose.

"Can I help you, young lady?" a voice asked from behind.

Rose jumped up to see Spiton holding a closed umbrella in a defensive fashion. She also noticed that she had become covered in dust. She projected a brown and gray silhouette.

"I tripped on you in the plane, didn't I?" deduced Spiton. "I thought that one of the seat cushions looked strangely pressed down. Are you a friend of Driftwood?"

"Yes," admitted Rose, too startled to lie.

"Well then, as I said before, can I help you?"

Rose was having difficulty guessing the servant's intentions. Spiton then knelt down on one knee and held up the umbrella like a sword.

"Allow me to properly introduce myself," he said mannerly. "My name is Sir Murph Magee, Magician, Knight and Spy Extraordinaire for The Order of the Good and True."

# Chapter Twenty-Three

Driftwood was quite relieved when Clara and Wilson returned to the hotel for the season of the long day. The tensions between her and Old Bart had not gone away. Over that summer she spent a lot of time with Wilson in the kitchen. She would allow only Clara to teach her and would communicate with Old Bart only if absolutely necessary. Towards the end of August, Driftwood approached her former mentor as he carved by the fireplace.

"Old Bart, I need to speak with you" she began.

"Have you come to disagree with what I'm

*carving?" he retorted.*

*"Old Bart, I came to tell you that I'm going to spend the winter with Clara in Aujuittuq."*

*"I do not think that is wise."*

*"Why not?"*

*Old Bart struggled to respond. He had never told Driftwood that he was trying to keep her hidden. This was information that he was not prepared to divulge.*

*"Your home is here," he justified.*

*"If I have another winter like the last one this will never again feel like my home."*

*"I won't allow you to go."*

*"I am not asking your permission. I am telling you."*

*Old Bart turned away. A small smile came across his face.*

What a self-confident girl I have raised, *he thought proudly.*

*"Very well," he finally replied.*

*In late September, Clara Kunuk and*

Driftwood traveled to Aujuittuq. It was a day's journey by boat to the southern end of Ellesmere Island.

They arrived at night to the Kunuk family home. It was a little house on the edge of the small settlement. Driftwood slept on the couch in the living room. The next morning she awoke to young children running about. Clara's nieces and nephews had come over. Driftwood spent the morning playing with the young kids. They journeyed behind the couch to fight dragons and climbed the treacherous staircase as lava poured down it. She enjoyed herself immensely. The last time she felt she had truly innocent fun was the scavenger hunt of her tenth birthday. That had been over five years ago. For the next day and a half, Driftwood contemplated only one concept – fun. Her goal was to find something fun to do.

Driftwood went out exploring. Aujuittuq had a population of one hundred and sixty-three. There were a few rows of houses, lodges *and trailers. It was dark except for a few street lights. She saw some young kids having fun in a playground. It had bars, swings and all sorts of climbing toys. The children were laughing as they crawled about.*

The playground does look like fun, *thought Driftwood*, but I want something more like grown-up fun.

*When she got to the edge of the settlement, she saw an igloo about a hundred metres away. She could see the glow of a fire come through around the building's bricks. As the white dome flickered Driftwood became more and more entranced. She had made a decision on what she would do for fun.*

*She would build an igloo and live in it for the winter.*

# Chapter Twenty-Four

"Harry, show Driftwood around some more while I tend to some business," commanded Hans.

"Do you like to have fun?" asked Harry of his new sister.

"Uh…I guess so," responded Driftwood, not entirely sure that she and Harry would think the same things were fun.

"Follow me," instructed Harry as he ran around to the side of the house. "Catch me if you can."

Harry was twenty-one years old but Driftwood felt that he acted more like a bratty twelve year old.

Harry had led them to a giant playground. There were sixteen tire swings, forty-five slides and monkey bars that formed many different shapes. There was a pool of plastic balls that was ten metres deep. Pipes, bridges, pulleys and beams adorned the structure. It was about nineteen times bigger than the playground in Aujuittuq, noted Driftwood. Harry climbed on excitedly. Driftwood couldn't resist herself and climbed on as well.

"This is the Galaxy Jungle 3000," boasted Harry. "The third Blekansit designed this one back when some Great Blekansit Products actually made people more physically active. That was before father realized that lazy, inactive people will spend more money on things they don't need."

Driftwood was getting more and more disturbed every time her father or brother spoke of the GBP business. They talked so brazenly about trying to get money from other people. However, Driftwood had to admit that the Galaxy Jungle 3000 was pretty fun.

"So what do you do most of the time, Harry?" inquired Driftwood.

"I play and I play," replied Harry, "and when I get bored of playing, I lie on the beach."

"Would the two of you like something to drink?" cried a voice from beside the gym.

"Ah, Spiton," observed Harry as he hung from a monkey bar, "what have you brought us?"

"Lemonade, dear sir," affirmed the Blekansit man-servant, "and I took the courtesy of bringing an apple juice for you, Madam Driftwood."

"Why, thank you," Driftwood said as she took the glass.

"Oh, and before I forget, madam, " he

continued, "I've made up a bedroom for you. It is on the third floor. I hope I've prepared it to your liking, Madam…"

The old man then stared straight at Driftwood, blinked with a grin and hinted, "There are some roses there for you."

Driftwood suddenly understood that Spiton knew about Rose. She decided to trust him. There was something about him that reminded her of Old Bart.

"Oh, of course, I think it is time for me to get settled," said Driftwood. "Thank you, Harry, for showing me your toys."

"Whatever, half-blood. Before you go I just want you to remember one thing," Harry said as he grabbed Driftwood by the hair and brought her ear close to his mouth.

"Yipe!" she squealed.

"He will always love me more," he whispered into her ear.

Harry let go of the hair and walked off

leaving behind his lemonade.

Driftwood followed the elderly butler up to her room on the third floor. When they got there she immediately noticed that there were no flowers in her room. She called out for her friend.

"Rose?"

There was no response.

"It seems that we have lost her, madam, she was with me when we approached you and Harold," said the old man. "I'm sure that she will find us up here soon. May I properly introduce myself?"

Rose was still down by the Galaxy Jungle 3000. She was trying to remember which bag was salt and which bag was sugar. It was very hard to tell with them both being as translucent as she was.

The old man knelt down in front of Driftwood and held up his serving tray as a shield.

"My real name is Sir Murph Magee, Magician, Knight and Spy Extraordinaire for the Order of the Good and True."

"You're Murph Magee, Old Bart's friend?" exclaimed Driftwood. "You're Swamp's grandfather? What are you doing here?"

"I have been working undercover in the GBP Corporation for many years. I have been Hans Blekansit's personal assistant for the last three years."

"Why have you been spying on the Blekansits?"

"Many years ago Old Bart, myself and The Laughing Man were all young magicians in New York City. Hermit, as The Laughing Man had begun calling himself, was beginning to view money as entirely evil. He focused much of his anger on GBP Corporation and other big businesses. I had run Camp Magee until my son was old enough to take over. Then I took up the Good and True cause. I have fought many beasts and demons that plague our world. My never-ending battle led me to infiltrate GBP Corporation. I have worked for many years to gain a position of trust. It now appears time to strike."

"You said you knew Old Bart from a long time ago?"

"Back then, Old Bart had basically gotten tired of most aspects of modern society. He decided to move to Ellesmere Island to escape the world. As luck would have it, he had inadvertently placed himself in a most important position."

"Why is that?"

"He was there to find you, Driftwood. He was escaping society to better understand its problems and in fate's funny way you floated up to him as a solution. I have a diary I want you to read. I think it will answer a lot of questions for you."

Murph Magee handed Driftwood the

diary that Rose had discovered earlier. Driftwood opened it to the first page article. She fixated on the photograph.

"Is this my mother?" she asked.

"Yes," confirmed the knightly sage.

A little tear formed in Driftwood's eye. It was the first picture of her mother she had ever seen.

Driftwood began reading the article. It was from the Emporia Gazette almost eighteen years ago.

**Local Woman wins Husband in National Contest.**

*Emporia, Kansas - Eva Wood has beat out fifty–one other contestants to win Hans Blekansit as her billionaire husband. From a swimsuit competition to who could eat monkey brains the fastest, Eva played hard every week this season to finally win her mate on the finale of the smash hit TV show* Fight for Love.

*The happy couple will begin their lives with Harold, Hans' four-year old son, at their exclusive mansion in the Grand Cayman Islands.*

The short article informed her that Harry was actually her stepbrother. She kind of felt good about that. It also told her how her parents had met. Some strange TV show about love. TV and love. Driftwood was quite disappointed that her parents had met in such an artificial way. She started to read the diary.

*Dear Diary,*

*I am quite excited as I get ready to go to Grand Cayman with my new husband. We will finally get to be alone together. Hans has been so charming and kind during the show that I'm sure he will be a dream to live happily ever after with.*

The next passage read:

*The mansion is spectacular. Every room is wonderful. I have become a princess. It is like all my dreams have come true. I felt so excited as Hans guided me around. We have just taken our last photo shoot for the television show. Soon, my new life begins.*

Driftwood read further on:

*Our first month together has been like a fairy tale. We have elegant dinners every night. We take long walks along the beach. We dance in our main hall to musicians from around the world that Hans has flown in at great expense. We have waltzed to The Vienna Orchestra and tangoed to an Argentinean gypsy band. Every morning he gives me a gift. Today I was given ten different types of rare orchid. Yesterday, the gift was delicious African chocolates. The day before that it was a magnificent Kimono dress from Japan.*

And on:

*Hans has been very busy for the last week. He has hardly spent any time with me. The gifts have stopped. Yesterday, I discovered a strange creature in a backyard pen that I hadn't noticed before. When I asked Hans about it he said it was called an Eaderion and was the "cornerstone of his empire." He then scolded me for going where I didn't belong. I don't know how he could have expected me to not discover the beast as it is so close to our house. It makes me wonder what else he has kept from me.*

And on:

*I fear this marriage may have been a horrible mistake. Hans has been nothing but cruel to me since the first month of being here has been over. He orders me around and says that my only duties are to tend to the house staff and care for Harry, who is quite a brat. It is like Hans has become someone else.*

And on:

*Things have worsened. Hans yells at me constantly. He says it's my fault when the other Eaderion in New York invents an unsuccessful product. I do not know how this could be, as I have not left our estate since our marriage began. Hans now spends most of his time with Harry as they torture the baby Eaderion in the backyard.*

And on:

*I am pregnant. This would have made me happy mere months ago but I have become so fearful of Hans's anger that I don't want to bring another child close to him. Harry is such a mean boy. I was such a fool to think that love could be found on a TV show.*

Until:

*Hans hit me today. I must leave him before he discovers I am to have his baby.*

Driftwood stood in silence as she read the last two sentences over and over again. Only this morning had she started to learn about her mother. Driftwood had since been exposed to many parts of her family. She was not very happy with most any of it and the second last sentence of her mother's diary made her actually, truly angry with her father. She now understood why her mother had fled to the far ends of the earth.

"Your mother went back to her family in Emporia but Hans somehow learnt about

Eva's pregnancy and followed her there," Murph Magee explained. "She fled further and further away as Hans tried in vain to retrieve her. He finally lost her trail in the Arctic Circle. That was when she drifted into Eureka to give birth to you. In respect of her wishes, Old Bart raised you in secret from her abusive husband."

Driftwood broke into tears. She was suddenly so proud and thankful that her mother had traveled so far to find a safe and good home for a child.

"I don't know what to say or do," sobbed Driftwood.

"I have a suggestion," replied a familiar voice. "Does 'Let's get the heck out of here' work for you?"

Twinkling and fading into view was Rose. Driftwood was so excited to see Rose that she gave the newly visible girl a great big hug.

"Oh, Rose, I'm so happy you're all right,"

she cried.

"We better go," suggested Rose as she pulled what looked like a tiny model of the Galaxy Jungle 3000 out of her pocket. "I decided to try out your shrinking potion. They're going to learn that something's up pretty soon."

"Rose, I can't believe you took that," exclaimed Driftwood.

"Well, I thought Camp Magee could use something like this," explained Rose. "Besides, I also gave Harry a little something."

Harry soon realized that he didn't have anything to do, which was never surprising. He decided to return to the Galaxy Jungle 3000 and do a few laps in the plastic ball pool. When he got there he was stunned to see a giant empty space where, mere moments ago, the gigantic gym had been. Someone had stolen the gym from him and this made him angry. To cool his temper he had a drink from the lemonade he had left behind. As he made his way to Driftwood, his prime suspect, he started to feel a bit tingly in his stomach. Suddenly, he couldn't walk any further as gas was building up inside him at an alarming rate. The pressure grew worse and worse. It was finally released with a fart. And then another fart. And then another. And another. Followed by more.

"When will this stop?" he asked aloud as he tried to walk and pass gas at the same time.

He was finding it somewhat difficult.

# Chapter Twenty-Five

Driftwood's first two igloos were not successes. The first one had walls that were too thin to support themselves. She had cut the blocks with her Swiss Army knife. Its blade was too short for the task. Clara then lent Driftwood a longer knife to cut the blocks. The second shelter had collapsed because the walls were curved in too soon. Driftwood tried not to let her failures discourage her.

The third igloo was quite a success. The blocks spiraled up in perfect formation towards the centre of the dome. It had a tunnel entrance and a raised snow bed. The cracks had all been filled with snow and Driftwood had even put in a piece of ice as a window to let in the light from the stars and moon.

Clara had given blankets to Driftwood for her to use for her bed. She had also provided matches, a flask of seal oil and part of a whales jawbone.

"Burn the oil in the jawbone to heat up your home," instructed Clara. "Be sure you have a hole up top so you don't burn up all your air."

Driftwood enjoyed burning some seal oil and watching the flames cast dancing light against the white walls of snow and ice. The heat from her body and the burning oil made her igloo quite a comfortable space.

As the winter continued, Driftwood learnt more skills of the Inuit. She went ice fishing on the frozen sea. She had convinced some reluctant Inuit men to take her out hunting for seals and walruses. Throat singing became a passionate pastime for a few weeks. She thought very *little of her magic training during her time in Aujuittuq. She had experimented with a couple of potions but had generally focused on surviving without spells and incantations in her self-made igloo. However, on one occasion, at bedtime, she had taken out her wand.*

*"You're a flame," she chanted as she waved her willow wand at her oil filled jawbone.*

*Nothing happened.*

*"You're a spark," she said with a faint glimmer of hope in her words.*

*Again, nothing happened.*

*"Do you need a hand, dear?" Clara asked as she poked her head into the igloo.*

*"I've run out of matches and was trying to light my oil with magic," Driftwood replied. "I was hoping that my wand would finally work."*

*"Ikkuma Tikipok," chanted Clara as she waved her hand over the jawbone.*

*A small flame suddenly grew from the oil providing light to the shelter.*

"Why can't I get my wand to do anything?" complained Driftwood. "And how come you don't even use a wand?"

"I have transferred the power of the tool into my own hands," answered Clara. "Perhaps one day you will do the same. Now, would you like to hear a story or is the woman you've become too old for such things?"

"I may be fifteen but I'll never be too old for your stories, Clara. Is it an old one?"

"It is an old story but it is new to you. Now, as I tell you this story I want you to look at the moon shining through your ice window and the flame of the jawbone as it dances before you."

Driftwood positioned herself appropriately. It had been quite a while since Clara had told her a new story.

"Many seasons ago," began Clara, "there was a young girl named Malina. She had a brother named Anningan. Anningan liked to pull on Malina's hair. He would sneak into her igloo, *quickly tug on her strands and run out. One time, Malina saw her brother as he approached and tried to escape his cruel clutch. She knocked over a lamp and got her hands covered in grease. As she fought away her brother she covered his face with the shiny, dark oil. Malina ran out of her igloo. Anningan quickly followed. Malina ran up to the sky and became the sun. Her brother followed her up there and became the moon. For half the year Malina disappears as she tries to escape her mean brother. As Anningan chases his sister in the sky, he gets thinner and thinner for four weeks until he has to disappear for three days to eat. He then always returns to the sky to continue his hunt."*

*"Clara, do you think I might have a brother?" asked Driftwood.*

*"Perhaps you do, dear, perhaps you do."*

*"If I do, I wish that he's nice."*

# Chapter Twenty-Six

"Driftwood!" screamed Harry. "I'm going to pull out your hair and stick it up your nose!"

Harry had taken to walking with his knees locked together in an effort to stop the never-ending farting. He was finding it difficult to get up the stairs. When he got to Driftwood's room he found the window open. He looked out to see Spiton, Driftwood and some other girl at the bottom of some vines. The trio was on the ground and running before Harry could even open his mouth.

"We have to get to the Eaderion," gasped

Driftwood as they ran. Murph was having a hard time keeping up.

"I will meet you at the shore, young ladies," he blustered. "There is something I must do inside."

The girls made their way to the animal's hole. They looked down to see the little creature looking up at them.

"What a cutie!" stated Rose. "You're not planning on doing to this one what you did to the big one, are you?"

"Oh no, Rose," answered Driftwood, "I plan on rescuing this wee thing from the torture and punishment it has had to endure from this family. Now, help me climb down."

Hans was up in his fourth floor office, looking out as the sun was setting on his tropical paradise. Now that he had a daughter he was contemplating how to adequately punish her for the destruction of his older Eaderion. The beast's death would cause delays in his production schedule until he could successfully accelerate the growth of his infant creature. Hans looked over to the chimera's pen. He was startled to see a young girl helping Driftwood out of the hole with the baby Eaderion under her arm.

"My beast!" he cried out. "She is taking the beast!"

Hans ran down the stairs to be greeted in the front hall by his trusted man-servant.

"Spiton, we must hurry," Hans wheezed as he stopped for air. "That bratty girl seems to be betraying me yet again."

"And with good reason," was the long time lackey's only response.

"Pardon me, Spiton?"

Murph Magee then made the sound one makes just before one is about to spit a big lugger.

"Haaaayuuk," Murph breathed in.

"Spiton, what is the meaning of this?"

184

Murph then turned his head.

"Piiitooo," was the only sound he made as an arc of gob came out of his mouth and landed on the three gold monuments of the Blekansit men.

"Spiton, how dare you try and spit on me!" screamed Hans.

"If I'd meant to hit you then you would have been hit," answered the old servant. "Now, watch what I've done."

Hans watched in horror as Murph's spit seemed to react with the statues. There was some bubbling, fizzing and screeching as the three gold figures shrunk until they were the size of a key chain.

"My statues!" yelled Hans. "All that gold reduced to nothing."

"Oh, I'll be able to enlarge them again when I'm far away from this place," said Murph as he scooped up the now-tiny replicas. "Now, 'Master', there is something I've been wanting to say to you for quite some time."

Murph stared Hans directly in the eye. He held up one hand between the two of them. His middle finger was pressing tensely against his thumb.

"All you do is want and want and want in the manner of an infant child," the old magician stated. "You consume without ever giving or thinking about others. Quite frankly, 'Master', you are a pig."

Murph snapped his fingers on the last word.

Hans grew a snout, his hands and feet became hooves and a curly tail grew from his behind.

"Oink! Oink! Oink!" he screamed in shock. Hans scurried around the front hall squealing in his new body.

Murph quickly made his way out the front door. He could see Rose and Driftwood by the shore. Driftwood had her hands stretched out into the ocean. Rose seemed to be struggling with something.

"Come on, little fella," said an annoyed Rose, "calm down. We're trying to rescue you."

The baby Eaderion was trying desperately to escape Rose's grip. Driftwood was not paying any attention. She was concentrating on the ocean. Her eyes were closed as she repeated the same word over and over.

"Yemaya, Yemaya, Yemaya," she chanted louder and louder each time. Driftwood and Rose were both too distracted to notice someone waddling like a penguin towards them.

"Did you think you were going to yell your way off this island?" asked Harry as he approached. "You know, for someone who is so good at messing with our business, you are equally good at getting caught."

"You haven't caught us yet," replied

Driftwood as she reached into her pack and grabbed her wand.

"You seem to be walking a bit slow, Harry," chimed in Rose between animal wrestling moves. "You should drink something for that."

"That was you? I'll make you pay!" he screamed as he ran towards Rose. Driftwood intercepted him and stuck her wand in his face.

"You're nothing but dust," she chanted. Harry tackled her.

"I'll show you dust," he responded as he pinned her down.

"You're a piece of dirt," she stated as she pointed the wand into his face.

"Can a piece of dirt do this?" replied Harry as he grabbed the willow wand and tore it into pieces.

Something unexpected happened to Driftwood. As the willow pieces fell onto her face she felt a surge of energy enter her like an epiphany. The flimsy wand had long been a distraction and had come to remind Driftwood of past inabilities. Its destruction was allowing her to forget her failures and clearly recognize her power. She suddenly understood the potential that she had at her fingertips. She had found her focus.

She waved one of her hands in front of Harry's face as she thought of the story of Anningan and Malina.

"You are moon rock," she said calmly.

Something happened.

"That's what you thi--"

Harry was interrupted as his hand suddenly became gray as a storm cloud. It turned rough and crumbly right before his eyes. The effect seemed to be moving up his arm.

"What is happening to me?" he screamed. "What have yo—"

Hans scurried around the front hall squealing in his new body

Harry had become a moonstone statue.

"Finally, he stopped breaking wind," quipped Rose as the Eaderion stuck a paw up her nose.

Murph had caught up with them. He helped Driftwood crawl out from under the statue that was her brother.

"Driftwood," inquired Rose, "what exactly is your plan? What were you doing before with that chanting?"

"I was calling for a ride," explained Driftwood as a geyser of water started to rise up from the ocean. A beautiful woman arose out of the top of the cascading pillar. She had gorgeous black skin and a long elegant, blue dress. Instead of feet she had a giant fin. She smiled and was welcoming when she spoke.

"I am Yemaya, sea goddess of African and Cuban waters. Why have you land creatures summoned me?"

# Chapter Twenty-Seven

Driftwood returned to the Toque and Mitt Inn in the spring of her fifteenth year after spending five months living in her igloo behind the Kunuk family home in Aujuittuq. It was her first time to return home after a long absence. Her heart was filled with memories as she walked by the picnic table. For some reason she had remembered the table to be bigger. Everything seemed a bit smaller to her.

As she walked into the Inn she was greeted by the familiar site of Old Bart whittling by the fire. She approached her guardian and mentor. They were very formal with their greetings of each other.

"You look stronger," Old Bart observed.

"I learnt many things while I was gone," Driftwood replied, "like how to icefish and how to make clothes out of animal skin."

"Did you work on your magic while you were gone?"

"Not very much. It was nice to take a break from it."

"Do you still want to become a magician?"

Driftwood had forgotten that being a magician had actually been a choice that she had made when back on top of Blacktop Mountain.

"Didn't you say on my fourteenth birthday that I already was a magician?" she reminded him.

"One never finishes becoming a magician," Old Bart lectured. "It is a path that requires a desire to never finish learning. There is no final exam. It is a lifetime of tests. Again, I ask you, do you still want to become a magician?"

"Of course," responded Driftwood although a part of her was not convinced of her answer.

In Aujuittuq, she had realized that there was a world of skills outside of magic that she could learn and excel at. Perhaps she was meant to do something else. She did not want to share her doubts with Old Bart. She decided instead to show him something.

"I've been working on a potion," she informed him. "Would you like to see it?"

"What does it do?" he inquired.

"Follow me," she replied as she walked outside.

Old Bart followed her.

When they got outside Driftwood took her Mason jar out of her pack and removed the lid, careful not to spill a drop of the contents.

"I just need to add some final ingredients and enchant the formula," she said as she took out her Swiss Army Knife, the bag of tea leaves and her flute.

*With her knife she scraped some lichen off of a rock. The strong fungi broke up into little grains as it was removed from its stone home. The lichen powder and a cut-up tea leaf were added to the clear liquid in the jar. She sat down and placed the jar a couple feet in front of her. She played a short song on her flute that she had composed. She then grabbed the jar, held it above her head and chanted:*

Potion magic potion
Find the way and use the how
Make the future happen quick
Bring it forward right now

*The brew suddenly changed to a dark, opaque color. She poured the black contents over some nearby rocks. The stones began to fizz.*

*Old Bart watched as the boulders were quickly eaten by lichen to become soil. A process that normally would take thousands and thousands of years happened in mere moments. From the soil grew a garden of willow trees in a matter of seconds.*

*"I have figured out a way to speed up time," the sorceress excitedly explained.*

*As Old Bart studied the branches of the newly created trees he did not look very excited. He looked quite stern. The trees all grew up and died in less than ten seconds. The small forest quickly produced a new generation of willow trees. This continued for many cycles, all in just a few minutes. Eventually, the last willow tree decomposed to leave nothing but dirt. The dirt blew away. Soon, all that was left was a giant hole where the rocks had been.*

*"Oops!" said the apprentice.*

*"Driftwood, you mustn't meddle with nature like this," rebuked Old Bart. "One must use caution and restraint when experimenting with cosmic power."*

*Driftwood's feelings of embarrassment and*

*failure returned like a flash flood. She chose her usual defense of attacking Old Bart.*

*"I can't do anything right with you," she snapped and stormed off to her room.*

*She locked her door. She cried and cried and cried. And cried.*

*Old Bart realized that something must be done. Driftwood had grown beyond his hotel. He needed a safe place for her to go and experience more of life. She needed to make friends. He went inside to the front desk of the Inn. He opened his address book, picked up the satellite phone and dialed.*

*"Hello, is this Marv Magee of Camp Magee? It is? My name is Old Bart, an old friend of your grandfather, Murph. I have a favor to ask. Are you looking to hire any more counselors for this summer?"*

# Chapter Twenty-Eight

Rose gawked with awe at the sea goddess as the Eaderion squirmed aggressively in her arms. Murph Magee knelt before the deity in an honorable fashion. Driftwood confidently addressed the mystical woman.

"I summoned you, Great Yemaya," Driftwood stated. "I have previously met your sister, Sedna, goddess of the Arctic waters."

"Oh, I've heard of you, dear child," Yemaya responded.

She waved her hands which seemed to cause her giant water pillar to lower. She was now close to the three humans.

"Sedna told me that you are an orphan of the waters," Yemaya tenderly noted. "Did you learn about your parents, young one?"

"I have learnt that my father is a despicable man and that my mother died as she saved me from him," Driftwood replied furiously.

"I can see why my sister Sedna took a liking to you," observed Yemaya. "You have similar anguish. However, I ask again, why have you summoned me?"

"I was hoping one of your mighty whales could carry us home," answered Driftwood.

"It shall be done," commanded Yemaya.

With a motion of her hand, a wave came and picked up the two girls, the old man and the strange animal. The wave dropped them onto the back of a giant whale.

"You will be taken to wherever you seek on the ocean waters," advised Yemaya. "Fare thee well, young girl, and give my regards to my sister Sedna."

With a mighty spout spurt the whale took off immediately. Yemaya returned to the ocean. Hans had scurried to the shore and was now oinking madly at his son. Harry, being made of moon rock, said nothing in return.

Rose was growing frustrated with the chimera flailing about in her arms.

"Uh, Drifty, can you help me out?" requested Rose. "I'm getting scratched and poked a lot over here."

Driftwood took the Eaderion into her arms. She began to pet it much like she would pet Bast the Cat. The Eaderion responded quite favorably, calmed down and began to sleep in Driftwood's arms. Driftwood smiled at the little creature.

"I think I'll call you Edie," she whispered gently to the magical monster.

The group was carried by the whale up the Atlantic Ocean and around the east side of North America. As they traveled, Driftwood asked Rose a question that had been avoided for quite a while.

"Rose, where is your home?" the young mage inquired.

"The truth is," answered Rose, "I don't have a home. Before I worked at the camp I was as homeless and hungry as those teenagers we met in New York. I grew up in an orphanage but it was a nasty, horrible place so I ran away when I was nine. I lived on the streets for seven years before I discovered Camp Magee. I've spent the last two summers working there but I lived in a cardboard box in Victoria during the winter between. I might return there for this winter. It's pretty warm in Victoria so living outside is not that bad."

Murph put his hand on Rose's shoulder. With his other hand he brought out the three tiny gold statues.

"I think that after I return to Camp Magee we might have enough money to run the camp all year and we could sure use your help, Rose," he said, "unless Driftwood wants these statues as a memento of her family."

Driftwood looked at the figures of her stepbrother, father and grandfather. She then noticed that she was still wearing her mother's necklace.

"I think the amulet will be memory enough. Take the gold from these statues and use it to help children," Driftwood requested as she looked at Rose. "Use it to help all children."

The whale went west of Greenland and into the Arctic Circle. It finally reached the shore of the Eureka Research Compound on Ellesmere Island.

Driftwood placed Edie on the rocky beach to crawl around. She then jumped back on the whale to say goodbye.

"Murph Magee, I want to thank you for your help in getting us away from Blekansit

Manor," Driftwood said with a bow. "You truly are an extraordinary magician, knight and spy."

"It has been a great and distinct pleasure, Lady Driftwood," responded Murph as he knelt down in his knightly fashion. "Give my regards to Old Bart when you see him."

Driftwood then looked at Rose. It was hard for both of them not to cry. Although they had known each other for less than eight weeks, they had become the best of friends and had shared in many wondrous adventures. They hugged each other tightly.

"Take care, Drifty," whispered Rose as she held back her tears.

"You, too," replied Driftwood, "I'll miss you."

"You're coming back to the camp next summer, aren't you?"

"Nothing could stop me," stated Driftwood as she jumped off the whale.

"You know," added Rose as she waved, "I really don't think you could be stopped from doing anything."

"You know," added Rose as she waved, "I really don't think you could be stopped from doing anything."

"Goodbye, Marianne," waved Driftwood.

"See you soon, Drifty," said Rose as tears fell from her eyes. No one had called her by her given name for many a year. The only time she had told it to Driftwood was when they first met.

The whale set off for the Pacific Ocean to make its way to the coast of British Columbia.

Driftwood and Edie made their way up to the Toque and Mitt Inn. They were greeted on the porch by Clara and by Wilson, who had just returned from New York. It was early September and the sun was setting on the hotel for the first time in quite a while. The long day of summer was about to end.

"Welcome back, dear," whispered Clara as she emotionally embraced Driftwood.

"Oh, Clara," cried Driftwood, "I have so much to tell you. I have learnt so much about who I am and what I can do."

"I know, child, and I will be here to listen whenever you want to talk."

Wilson then chimed in, "Hey, Driftwood, what's with the ugly dog?"

Driftwood left Edie with Clara, Wilson and Bast, who was cautiously approaching and analyzing the new pet. Driftwood walked through the doors of the Inn for the first time in two months. Never before had she been so nervous to see her mentor. She let out a quick 'oomp' and 'ah' in hopes of getting advice on what to do when she saw him.

Walking into the tavern she saw Old Bart at his familiar spot by the fire. He was about to take a bite out of an apple. Driftwood calmly waved one of her hands in the direction of Old Bart.

"It is an orange," she serenely incanted.

Old Bart took his bite and was surprised to have a bitter taste in his mouth. His face was squirted with orange juice. He started to chuckle as he wiped away the sticky substance from his eyes.

"So, I see you have learnt how to find your focus," the old teacher observed as he opened his eyes. "My goodness, how you've grown."

"I've been gone for over two months," Driftwood pointed out.

She was trying to remain composed but was finding it difficult as she looked into the eyes of her lifelong guardian and teacher. The angst and anger that she had so often felt before seemed ridiculous to her now.

"It feels like we've been apart for over two years," Old Bart said as he began to sob.

"Oh, Old Bart," Driftwood cried tearfully as she ran into her guardian's arms. "I am so sorry for how I acted whenever you tried to teach me these last two years."

"It's all right, Driftwood," whispered Old Bart. "I, too, must apologize. There comes a time in some people's lives when they can learn better as their own teacher. You have reached that time."

"I have?"

"You have proven it with how spectacularly you handled yourself when you went to Camp Magee and on your quest afterwards. You have saved many children from the hypnotic spell of video games. You have removed the mystical Eaderion's lineage from Great Blekansit Products, rendering your evil father's company practically powerless."

"My idea is if we raise Edie to be good and true, she might actually invent things that can help humans."

"Wise thinking, Driftwood, and time there will be for that. Now, I know you are an independent adult but are you too old to go down to the water and skip rocks towards the sunset with an old fart like me?"

"Not at all," replied Driftwood as she held her parent's hand. "That sounds like a lot of fun."

# The End